P9-EJU-015

Death *of an* Honest Man

More Hamish Macbeth Mysteries by M. C. Beaton

Death of a Ghost
Death of a Nurse
Death of a Liar
Death of a Policeman
Death of Yesterday
Death of a Kingfisher
Death of a Chimney Sweep
Death of a Valentine
Death of a Witch
Death of a Gentle Lady
Death of a Maid
Death of a Dreamer
Death of a Bore
Death of a Poison Pen
Death of a Village
Death of a Celebrity
Death of a Dustman
Death of an Addict
Death of a Scriptwriter
Death of a Dentist
Death of a Macho Man
Death of a Nag
Death of a Charming Man
Death of a Travelling Man
Death of a Greedy Woman
Death of a Prankster
Death of a Snob
Death of a Hussy
Death of a Perfect Wife
Death of an Outsider
Death of a Cad
Death of a Gossip
A Highland Christmas

M. C. BEATON

Death *of an* Honest Man

GC

GRAND CENTRAL
PUBLISHING

NEW YORK   BOSTON

This book is a work of fiction. Names, characters, places, and incidents are the product of the author's imagination or are used fictitiously. Any resemblance to actual events, locales, or persons, living or dead, is coincidental.

Grand Central Publishing
Hachette Book Group
1290 Avenue of the Americas, New York, NY 10104

grandcentralpublishing.com
twitter.com/grandcentralpub

First Edition: February 2018

Grand Central Publishing is a division of Hachette Book Group, Inc. The Grand Central Publishing name and logo is a trademark of Hachette Book Group, Inc.

The publisher is not responsible for websites (or their content) that are not owned by the publisher.

The Hachette Speakers Bureau provides a wide range of authors for speaking events. To find out more, go to www.hachettespeakersbureau.com or call (866) 376-6591.

Library of Congress Cataloging-in-Publication Data

Names: Beaton, M. C., author.

Title: Death of an honest man / M.C. Beaton.

Description: First Edition. | New York; Boston: Grand Central Publishing,

2018. | Series: A Hamish Macbeth mystery; [33]

Identifiers: LCCN 2017037492| ISBN 9781455558315 (hardback) |
ISBN 9781478902492 (audio download) | ISBN 9781478950257 (audio book) |
ISBN 9781455558339 (ebook)

Subjects: LCSH: Macbeth, Hamish (Fictitious character)—Fiction. | Police—Scotland—Highlands—Fiction. | Murder—Investigation—Fiction. | BISAC: FICTION / Mystery & Detective / Police Procedural. | FICTION / Mystery & Detective / Traditional British. | GSAFD: Mystery fiction.

Classification: LCC PR6053.H4535 D349 2018 | DDC 823/.914—dc23

LC record available at https://lccn.loc.gov/2017037492

ISBNs: 978-1-4555-5831-5 (hardcover), 978-1-4555-5833-9 (ebook)

Printed in the United States of America

LSC-H

10 9 8 7 6 5 4 3 2 1

To Chief Purser Bobbie Milne
and all the crew of the
Hebridean Princess, *with affection.*

Death *of an* Honest Man

CHAPTER ONE

A little sincerity is a dangerous thing,
and a great deal of it is absolutely fatal.

—Oscar Wilde

The day had started out well for Sergeant Hamish Macbeth. It was high summer with golden light bathing the little village of Lochdubh, situated in Sutherland in the northwest of Scotland. The air was pure and fresh and scented with pine from the forest on the other side of the sea loch. A yacht sailed in and the *putt putt putt* of the donkey engine was the only sound to break the silence of the early morning.

Hamish's beat was the whole of the county. He was helped by his amiable although clumsy sidekick, Police Constable Charlie Carter. Hamish was tall but Charlie was even taller, and so, after breaking too many things at the police station, Charlie had found himself a little apartment in the basement of the Tommel Castle Hotel.

He had joined Hamish for breakfast and now both men were leaning against the seawall, gazing dreamily at the water.

"There's a new chap over at Cnothan," said Charlie. "Are we going to see him?"

"May as well," said Hamish. "Know anything about him?"

"Not a lot. Name's Paul English. Retired banker."

"Oh, dear," said Hamish. "Cnothan's a sour place. Better give him a welcome."

"Will we take the dogs?"

"I suppose so," said Hamish reluctantly. He had two dogs, one called Lugs because of his large ears and a little poodle called Sally. But somehow, since the day he had released his wild cat, Sonsie, into the wild cat sanctuary at Ardnamurchan, he could not feel the same affection for the dogs.

* * *

"I forgot to ask you," said Hamish as he negotiated the police Land Rover down Cnothan's main street, "where this Paul English lives."

"You go along the waterfront and it's a bittie along. One of thae Victorian villas, meant to look like a Swiss chalet but ends up looking like something out of Charles Addams."

Hamish detested Cnothan and thought it the sourest village in the Highlands, but even in this place, with the sun sparkling on the loch, nothing could dampen his mood.

That was until he met Paul English.

For after Paul had ushered them into his front living room and said his first words, Hamish thought he had never come across anyone before so armoured in smugness. His first words were, "You gay men are always dyeing your hair." Hamish's hair was deep red.

"It iss my own colour," said Hamish, his highland accent becoming more sibilant as it always did when he was angry.

Paul shrugged his fat shoulders.

"At least I do have hair," said Hamish, for Paul was bald. "Welcome to the neighbourhood."

Paul English was a tubby man with a smug face. His very eyebrows looked smug. He had a small, pursed mouth. His accent was from somewhere in the Lowlands.

"We'll be off then," said Hamish.

"No need to dash off. I was just about to have coffee. Please join me."

Give him a chance, said the voice of Hamish's conscience.

"Thank you," he said.

Charlie lowered himself carefully onto the sturdiest chair he could see. Hamish looked around the room. Sterile, was his first thought. The carpet was fitted, a sort of mud-brown colour to match the mud-brown linen covers on the sofa and two armchairs. There were no curtains at the windows. Instead there were dark-green blinds, half drawn down. A glass coffee table was in front of the sofa and an ugly old-fashioned two-bar electric fire was set in front of the fireplace. There were no books or pictures. The ceiling was high. A glass bowl with one lightbulb inside and the corpses of flies hung from the centre.

The wind suddenly soughed through the weather outside with a mournful whistling sound.

Paul picked up a brass bell in the shape of a crinolined lady from the coffee table and rang it. The door slowly opened and an elderly woman came in wearing a droopy dress and a flowered pinafore. Women's Lib has a hard time in some places in the far north of Scotland making even the slightest impression. So the pinafore was of the sort you see in old photographs, covering nearly the whole body.

"Coffee," ordered Paul.

"What is auld Granny Dinwiddy doing working for you?" exclaimed Hamish. "She's got arthritis and is well into her eighties."

"People charge too much round here so I always go for the one who needs the money most."

"So, she is paid below the minimum wage."

"Did I say that? How long have you two been a pair?"

Charlie rose to his feet. He picked up Paul as if he weighed little more than a child and said, "Hamish and I have been together for a bit, but I often fancy a wee bit on the side."

"Oh, put him down," said Hamish. "That one couldnae see a joke if it jumped out o' his soup and bit him in the bum."

Charlie dropped Paul back in his chair and patted him on his bald head.

"Get out of here," raged Paul. "I find you disgusting."

"Be verra careful," cautioned Hamish, "or I'll have you for a hate crime."

"I speak as I find," shouted Paul.

"Aye, wi' no thought for anyone else's feelings. Good day."

"What a wee horror," commented Charlie as they both climbed into the police Land Rover.

Hamish did not start the engine but stared bleakly out at the steel-grey waters of the man-made loch round which nothing grew except a few stunted trees and, as Eliot said of Rannoch Moor, no birds sang.

"I don't like him," said Hamish at last. "There's death in the air."

"Och, c'mon, Hamish. Unless you think he's going to slave-drive Mrs. Dinwiddy into an early grave."

Hamish shrugged. "I'm imagining things. This village aye gives me the creeps. Let's get back to the station and have a fry-up. I'll call on Granny Dinwiddy later."

"Stop off at Patel's," said Charlie. "He's got venison sausages. You never take the dogs with you now like you did when you had the wild cat."

"They're fine," said Hamish. "They've got the flap on the door so they can come and go. Better that than cooped up in a vehicle."

Hamish often felt like a little piece of his heart had left with the large cat. The cat's replacement, the little white-haired poodle called Sally, did nothing to stop Hamish's feelings of loss, although Lugs seemed delighted with this new companion. Hamish sometimes felt Lugs was being, well, unfaithful and then cursed himself for being so sentimental.

They found the normally placid Mr. Patel in a rage. "I am Scottish," he shouted.

"So you are," said Hamish. "Who's been saying otherwise?"

"A wee fat mannie. Came in here yesterday and said, 'You immigrants do well for yourself.' Says I, 'Look, mac, I'm Scottish.' He sneers, 'Oh, yeah, where did you get that tan? You're as brown as my boots. You natives should go back where you came from.'"

Hamish's hazel eyes gleamed. "Did anyone hear him?"

"No, the shop was empty at the time."

"Charlie," said Hamish. "Take a statement from him."

* * *

Over a mammoth breakfast, Hamish said, "We can try to arrest him for a hate crime but we need proof. Oh, there's the door. What now?"

He opened the door and the small figures of the Currie sisters scuttled in: spinster twins, dressed in identical camel-hair coats with identical glasses and identical permed hair. Nessie shouted, "Arrest him!"

"Who?" asked Hamish.

"Thon Mr. English. Do you know what he said to Jessie?"

"Said to Jessie," chorused her sister who always repeated

the last line of anyone's conversation, like Browning's brave thrush trying to recapture that first fine careless rapture.

"Tell me."

"He said she needed to go to a psychiatrist and get a mind of her own."

"Of her own," sighed Jessie.

"I cannae arrest him for that. Has he upset anyone else?"

"He told Mr. Wellington that his sermons were boring, but it was what he said to Mrs. Wellington!"

Hamish ignored the Greek chorus that was her sister. "He said she was fat and should go on a diet because she was a bad example."

"Gets worse," commented Hamish. "Any more?"

"Mr. Maclean."

"Archie? What did he say?"

"He laughed in his face and said he looked shrink-wrapped in a tweed suit."

Archie the fisherman's wife boiled all his clothes with the result that they were always too short and too tight.

"Don't worry, ladies," said Hamish. "I'll go back to see him as soon as I finish eating."

It wasn't only this Paul English who should watch what he said, thought Hamish, as Nessie's voice from outside came back to him. "Got to eat, eh? That's why they call them pigs."

"Well, Charlie," said Hamish, "we'd better pull him in. We can charge him with a hate crime because of Mr. Patel's statement and that can be enough to go with."

"I s'pose," said Charlie, looking out of the window. "Mind you, it's the grand day and the games are on at Drumnadrochit. We could always arrest him in the evening."

"Aye, the silly sod isn't worth wasting the day on. What brought him up here?"

"He's been heard to say, quality of life."

"Another drunk, probably. They aye hae this dream o' Bonnie Prince Charlie and Mel Gibson's view on history and the only romance they ever find is at the bottom of a whisky glass. Next winter should see him off. Nothing like a highland winter for bringing a bad case of the rehabs."

Hamish insisted on washing up and told Charlie to go outside and stay there until he had finished. Sometimes it seemed as if clumsy Charlie could break dishes by just looking at them.

When he rejoined Charlie, he noticed his dogs in the back. He felt a tinge of sadness. He hadn't heard from Elspeth Grant although he often saw her reading the news on television from Glasgow. They had spent a wonderful weekend together but nothing had come of it although at first he had phoned almost every day. She always said she was too busy to see him, and at last, he had given up calling.

"What we ought to do," said Charlie as they drove out of Lochdubh and up over the hills, "is introduce thon scunner, Blair, to Paul English and see what happens."

Hamish laughed. "You mean like light the touch paper and retire? Great idea. I'm still worried about Blair. I know he's capable of murder and he hates me." Detective Chief Inspector Blair was the bane of Hamish's life. And Hamish knew Blair had caused the death the previous year of someone who was a threat to him.

* * *

Blair climbed the stairs to speak to his boss, Superintendent Daviot. Helen, the secretary, was just replacing the phone. "Macbeth again," she said.

The detective's bloodshot eyes shone with malice. "What's he been up to?"

"There's a newcomer over at Cnothan called Mr. English who claims Macbeth and the other policeman insulted him and the policeman also made a pass at him."

"I'd better go and see him," crowed Blair. "But I'll just be having a wee word with the boss first."

* * *

Blair had been warned to be careful about mentioning homosexuality in these fragile days, but he regarded homosexuals with that sort of deep contempt that only a man whose sexuality might be in question could feel.

He had decided to adopt a sort of hail-fellow-well-met attitude and so he shook hands with Paul and said with a chortle, "Got a pass made at you by a shirtlifter, hey?"

"What are you talking about?" demanded Paul.

"Macbeth's sidekick. Big fairy called Charlie."

"I shall have to report your politically incorrect remarks to your superior officers," said Paul, beginning to enjoy himself.

"Who do you think you're dealing with, laddie? I amn't some teuchter like Macbeth. But I'll admit he needs taking down and so I'll get a statement from you." Blair sat down without being asked.

Paul began to feel a prickling of unease. Who were this man's superiors going to believe? Himself? Or one of their own, namely Hamish Macbeth.

"I would prefer not to discuss the matter," said Paul. "No charges."

"Whit?" demanded the enraged Blair. "I come out here to the back o' beyond and then you decide you don't want to speak? Get this, laddie, I will be charging you with wasting police time if you don't get on with it and make a statement."

Paul looked at Blair's face, which was a network of broken veins. "You drink too much," he said.

"What's that got to dae wi' Charlie making a pass at ye?"

"As you have the face of a heavy drinker, I want to be sure I am not wasting my time making a statement. You might leave here and go to the nearest bar and forget about the whole thing."

"Keep yer damn personal remarks to yourself," shouted Blair. "How did Charlie Carter make a pass at ye?"

"He picked me up and laid hands on me."

"On yer bum?"

"He patted me on the head."

"In retaliation to what?"

"I simply asked if he and the other officer were a pair."

"Michty me. And you expect me to make a case out o' that?"

"Oh, do your duty, man." Paul sniffed the air. "You've been drinking already. What is the name of your superior officer?"

He took a step back as Blair stood up and advanced on him. "See here," said Blair. "Any mair reports agin the police and it'll be the end of you."

"Are you threatening me?"

"You report me, you scunner, and I will hae you for wasting police time."

The door of Paul's living room opened and Granny Dinwiddy walked in. "Will you be wanting coffee or tea?" she asked.

"No, but make sure you make a good job of cleaning the kitchen," snapped Paul.

When the woman had left, Blair said, "Your maid's too damn auld tae be a skivvy. Do you at least pay her the minimum wage?"

"That is my business," said Paul, becoming flustered.

He tried to bar the way but Blair nipped round him and into the kitchen where he could be heard asking Granny Dinwiddy how much she was being paid. Now, Granny Dinwiddy was only being paid five pounds an hour and she knew it should be seven pounds, fifteen pence, but she was expert at thieving stuff from the kitchen so that Paul would never notice: a teabag or two, sugar cubes, siphon off a little bit of whisky, cuts of meat shaved off what Paul got from the butcher, and occasionally stealing a note out of his wallet when he had fallen asleep. So to Blair's great disappointment, she said she was paid the minimum wage.

Paul overheard her and sighed with relief, but, he reflected, because of her age, people would think him a sort of slave driver, so as soon as Blair had stomped his way out, he told Granny Dinwiddy that her services were no longer needed.

"Yes, they are, or I will tell them what you are actually paying me," she protested.

"I give you cash. You've no proof. Who are they going to believe? Me, or a senile old fool like you?"

She fished in her apron pocket and held up a small tape recorder. "They'll believe this."

He made to snatch it out of her hand but she seized a marble rolling pin and struck him on the nose. He reeled back, blood running down his face. "I'll sue you," he yelled. "I'm off to the doctor. Don't be here when I get back."

* * *

Hamish was leaning on the seawall that evening, looking dreamily at the loch, when he heard himself being hailed by Angela Brodie, the doctor's wife.

"Someone gave Paul English a nasty dunt on the nose," she said. "He claims he walked into a cupboard."

"He's insulted everyone I can think of," said Hamish. "One of them was bound to crack. Has he insulted you?"

"Oh, yes, he came round with a book for me to sign. He said, 'Put down: To Paul, with apologies for writing this brainless pap.' So I wrote 'To Brainless Paul' and he cursed and yelled. There must be something really badly wrong with him. Do you think he's one of those people who are too frightened to commit suicide so they try to goad someone into killing them?"

"Mr. Smug? No. Not for a moment. Actually, I am taking a run up there. I'm sure he's underpaying Granny Dinwiddy. What on earth is the woman's proper name?"

"It's Maggie Dinwiddy and she's as old as Methuselah."

* * *

But when Hamish arrived at the cottage, Paul said that Mrs. Dinwiddy had gone home. His nose was taped and bandaged and he sounded like Kipling's elephant. "Ah fyredd 'er," he said.

"Fired her, did you? That means you were probably paying her cheap," said Hamish. "I'll go and ask her."

Paul had pale-green eyes like sea-washed glass. A flicker of malice shot through them. "Good 'uck."

Hamish drove down to the waterfront to a small cottage where he knew Maggie Dinwiddy lived with her daughter.

But her daughter, a widow called Holly Bates, said her mother hadn't come home. Hamish began to worry. Paul had looked so maliciously smug. Had he done something to her?

* * *

After two days, Hamish finally reported Maggie Dinwiddy as a missing person and said she may have come to harm. Paul seemed amused at all the police questions until it began to dawn on that brain of his, which was not one bit as intelligent as he thought it was, that he was suspected of murder. He reluctantly admitted he had paid for Maggie to go on a cruise. He supplied the name of the travel agency and the shipping line.

Maggie was contacted and said that—God bless the man—he had paid for this holiday out of the goodness of his heart, and that was all they could get out of her. Only Hamish guessed that Paul had been blackmailed by the cunning old fright.

All his smugness and confidence restored, Paul beamed on the police. That was until Detective Chief Inspector Blair charged him with perverting the course of justice and had him driven to police headquarters and dumped in a cell. Only after twenty-four miserable hours was he able to hire a lawyer who promptly got him out on bail, said he would defend him in court, then mentioned his fee and Paul, ever the cheapskate, spluttered that he would defend himself.

* * *

Hamish felt uneasy. There was something nasty about the whole thing. Paul had probably paid Maggie in cash so it would be only his word against hers. He decided to pay another visit to her daughter, Holly. Why hadn't Holly said anything about the cruise? Surely her mother would have told her.

But Holly stoutly said that her mother had said nothing about a cruise and all her clothes were in the wardrobe so what else was she supposed to think? Hamish asked to see the clothes and sure enough, the admittedly meagre wardrobe seemed to be intact. The phone rang and Holly went through to the living room to answer it. Hamish began to search through the pockets of the clothes, hoping for some clue, until his hands closed on the little tape recorder. He heard Holly coming back and put the recorder in his own pocket.

He was to curse himself afterwards and wish that he had simply given Holly a receipt for it.

Back at the police station, he was about to switch it on when Charlie came lumbering in, tripped over Lugs, and crashed down on the table, sending cups and plates flying.

Hamish helped him up and together they cleaned up the mess. "Now," said Hamish, "sit yourself down, take a deep breath, and tell me what's bothering you."

Charlie carried forward a stout oak chair, especially kept for him, and eased his bulk into it.

"I'm not enjoying being a policeman any mair, Hamish."

"Has anything happened?"

"It's thon scunner, Blair. Yesterday, you mind, you sent me back to Maggie's daughter but Blair was there and he was making her cry, shouting and yelling. So I picked him up and put him outside of the front door and locked it. So I'm to be charged with laying hands on a superior officer."

"It's all right, Charlie. I'll go and see Holly Bates. She'll say Blair frightened her and she'll stand up for you."

"No, she won't, Hamish."

"Whit?"

"Aye. I thought o' that and went back when the coast was clear and she point-blank refused to help me. Said she'd take Blair to court for police harassment and get money out o' the police to shut her up."

"There's something awfy fishy about thon pair. Wait! I took a tape recorder out o' one o' Maggie's pockets. She had left all her clothes behind, which means she not only got a cruise out o' Paul but new clothes as well. Help yourself to a dram and pour me one and we'll hae a listen."

"That's not even the minimum wage," came Maggie's voice.

Paul: "Like it or lump it."

Maggie: "I need the money and that's a fact."

"Is that all?" asked Charlie.

"Maybe there's something later on," said Hamish. "Oh, here we are!"

Maggie's jeering voice: "Get on all right at the doctor?"

"Why are you still here?"

Maggie: "I thocht we might come to an agreement afore I go to the police."

Paul: "What agreement, you old hag. No, get back. I'll listen."

Maggie: "I want new clothes and a two-week cruise to the Norwegian fjords and I want it now. Take me to the travel agency in Strathbane *now* or off I go to the polis. Or I'll maybe break yer heid the next time."

"I'll take this to Blair," said Hamish. "This gets him off the hook. What a pair! Oh, crivens. I just lifted this recorder. Now I have to go back and pretend to find it. And I'll bet she asks for a search warrant."

But to Hamish's relief, Holly smiled and let him look through the clothes again, but she let out a sharp exclamation when he held out the recorder and said he would give her a receipt for it.

"That's private property," she yelled. But Hamish merely smiled as he wrote out a receipt.

* * *

On board the Norwegian cruise ship, Maggie received a frantic call from her daughter about the tape recorder. Her companion on deck, an equally elderly lady, listened as Maggie shouted, "Get rid of him somehow."

"What is it, honey?" she asked when Maggie rang off.

"Oh, jist family," said Maggie.

"Oh, aren't they always just such a problem, honey," said her American companion, old Mrs. Merriweather. "Why, I do but mind…"

Maggie tuned her out. Oh, to be able to disappear! But as Mrs. Merriweather droned on about how too terribly sad it was to outlive your family, punctuating each sentence with a wave of her diamond-encrusted fingers, Maggie began to listen and look. People never really look at the very old, she thought. I mean, the number of times on this cruise the captain's called me by her name must be about fifty.

* * *

"She's what?" shouted Hamish two days later.

Holly's voice choked with sobs came over the line. "She jumped overboard and it's because I told her about the police harassment."

While she sobbed and accused, Hamish thought of crocodile tears and when he estimated she had wept a whole set of luggage, he simply put the phone down.

He whistled to his pets and drove up to the Tommel Castle Hotel to call on his sidekick in his flat in the basement. Charlie listened to Hamish's complaint and said, "You know what's been bothering me. If Maggie was blackmailing Paul, well, look at it this way, I've a feeling she and that daughter of hers must have done something like it before. There's another thing that's been bothering me. I don't think cheating auld Granny out o' the minimum wage was enough for a new wardrobe of clothes and a cruise. I think she and her daughter had something else on him."

"I wish we could get a search warrant."

"Maybe we could do it like this," said Charlie. "They're bound to find the body—well, let's hope they find the body. It'll be shipped back and there'll be a funeral. You go and I'll break in and have a wee keek."

Hamish looked at him with affection. Charlie was a policeman after his own heart.

CHAPTER TWO

She was poor but she was honest,
Victim of a rich man's game.
First he loved her, then he left her,
And she lost her maiden name.
It's the same the whole world over,
It's the poor wot gets the blame,
It's the rich wot gets the gravy.
Ain't it all a bleedin' shame!

—Military song, First World War

Paul English did not know it was to be his last night on earth. He never thought of the people at the receiving end of his much-prided honesty as victims. He told himself he was "putting them straight." He had led a pretty isolated life after Maggie had biffed him with the rolling pin and blackmailed him into that cruise. But the news that she had jumped overboard acted on his spirits like a bottle of the best wine.

He decided to run over to Lochdubh and find out if that stupid policeman had any news of Maggie's body being found. The locals all knew that the front door of the police station had been sealed shut with damp for ages and they all knew to use the kitchen door so Hamish, hearing a thunderous knocking at the front door, wondered who it could be. Had Paul remained quiet, then Hamish would have opened the door, but Paul shouted, "Come on, man. I haven't all night."

Charlie had developed a great affection for the poodle and had taken Sally off with him to the Tommel Castle Hotel. So Hamish quietly opened the kitchen window and lifted Lugs out onto the grass at the back and then squeezed his lanky frame out the window as well. He walked Lugs up through his small herd of sheep and on up to the peat stacks where he finally sat down and gazed up at the blazing stars overhead. Under his feet and under the peat still to be cut lay some of the oldest rock in the world. That and the combination of some Neolithic ruins to one side and the pitiless stars above gave him a superstitious shiver. There was nothing like the county of Sutherland for reminding petty humans that they were only renters on this planet and Landlord Earth could evict them anytime it chose.

He patted Lugs on the head, wondering why the dog did not seem to miss the poodle. Lugs had shown no sign of missing Sonsie, the wild cat, either. "Maybe you're a wee chauvinist pig," said Hamish.

"Who are ye calling a pig, ye daft gowk."

Hamish stared at his dog in alarm. "Did you just speak?"

"Aye, and you'd better get on down tae the pub. They're going to give thon Mr. English a ducking in the harbour."

"Who's there?" said Hamish.

"It's me, Willie Gordon."

"What are you doing up here, Willie?"

"Escaping from the wife."

Hamish set off running with great loping strides. He ran round the side of the police station and out onto the waterfront in time to hear Paul screaming, "Put me down."

Hamish usually had a soft lilting highland voice but it was a stentorian yell that sounded along the waterfront. "Police. Put him down *now!*"

Four men dropped Paul and disappeared into the blackness. Paul struggled to his feet and started to berate Hamish for not having arrested his assaulters. To his fury, Hamish twisted his own arm up his back and marched him back into the pub where he asked the barman, "How much did Mr. English have to drink?"

"Four double malts," said the barman.

"I am taking your car keys, Mr. English," said Hamish.

"Over my dead body."

Hamish kicked Paul's legs from under him, twisted him over and put handcuffs on him, dragged him to his feet, and fished in his pockets until he found Paul's car keys.

"I am taking you to the station," said Hamish, "where you will be locked in a cell until I consider you sober enough to drive. But first you will wait quietly here until I fetch a breathalyser and then take a statement from the barman, Forfar Timson. Keep an eye on him, Forfar."

In the station, Hamish suddenly could not remember where he had stacked the breathalysers until he remembered they were in a chest behind the freezer in the henhouse. He at last secured a kit and made his way back to the pub. Forfar, nicknamed Furry, was holding a towel to his bleeding nose and of Paul, there was no sign.

"What happened?" demanded Hamish.

Furry removed a blood-soaked towel and said, "Didnae the cheil gie me a dunt on the nose? Then he laughs in my face and walks off."

"With the handcuffs still on?"

"Aye."

Hamish set off at a run. Paul's car was still outside the pub.

There is no pollution in the far north of Scotland and so the combination of starlight and bright moonlight lit up the empty road ahead. Hamish roused Charlie to help in the search. They got into Charlie's old car and set out in the direction of Cnothan. They ranged the countryside until the sky paled, and when the sun rose at four in the morning, there was no sign of Paul and his house appeared to be empty.

* * *

His eyes gritty with lack of sleep, Hamish had to inform headquarters, and soon reinforcements had arrived.

Had Paul lived in any other highland village but Cnothan, Hamish would have had a list of everyone he knew and everyone he had talked to. But Cnothan was closed and secretive. He knew from past experience that a succession of slammed doors was all he was likely to get. He and Charlie met at a café in the main street.

"They call places like this greasy spoons in America," said Hamish, "but usually they turn out to be smart diners whereas this dump deserves the name. I gather you've had no luck?"

"I may have one thing," said Charlie. "If you are no' going to eat that bun, I'll have it."

"Go ahead," said Hamish, pushing his plate over.

"Slike 'is," mumbled Charlie.

"For heffen's sake, man, chew, swallow, and then speak."

Charlie gulped down a piece of bun and said, "A wee birdie telt me that himself had a mistress."

"Paul! What demented female did he lure into his bed?"

"Maisie Walters."

"The only Maisie Walters I know of is the Reverend Maisie Walters and she's the minister at the kirk here."

"Must be nonsense then," said Charlie gloomily. "It was a wee lassie that telt me. Only about nine years old. Fairy McSporran. Probably laughing about it wi' her horrible wee friends."

"Describe what she told you," ordered Hamish.

"I was going up to the kirk because I thought there might be some ladies there, cleaning the brass or whatever the volunteers do. But there was just this wee girl, kneeling and praying."

"In a kirk! She'll be damned as a papist if anyone catches her. Oh, I know. That film *The Passionate Nun* is showing at the community hall. I suppose all the lassies will want to be nuns until the next movie."

"Fairy heard me and got to her feet. She says, 'You must help me. Mrs. Walters is going to hell.' So I says, 'Why?' And she says that Mrs. Walters has had 'carnival knowledge' of Mr. English. I guessed she meant carnal knowledge and I said, 'You mustn't tell stories.'" Charlie took another bite of bun and gazed dreamily out at the main street. Hamish stared at him in amazement. How could the man drift off like that when he might have a hard bit of information?

Hamish did not know that Charlie was sick of being a policeman and escaped into his mind back to his home in South Uist in the Outer Hebrides.

Charlie blinked and then said, "Where was I? Oh, yes. So, I told her it was dangerous to make up stories like that but she said she often played in the church and one day she was in the kitchen—they have one because tea is sometimes served after the service—when the minister and Mr. English came in and she said they dropped their bottom clothes and began to grunt and heave. She told her big brother who hopes one day to be a minister and he told her that she couldn't have seen anything like that because it would mean Mr. English was having carnival knowledge of Mrs. Walters and that couldn't be the case because they weren't married."

"You know, Charlie, there's an awful ring of truth about all this. Let's go and have a chat to Mrs. Walters."

Mrs. Walters lived in a drab pebble-dashed bungalow which served as a manse. A brick path led up to the front door between regimented flower beds where the plants were so evenly placed and so upright, it was as if they had been ordered to stand to attention.

Hamish knocked on the door. It was abruptly opened by Mrs. Walters herself, who was much as Hamish remembered her to be: hair scraped back, thick glasses, thin mouth, dumpy figure, and no bra because her breasts were lumped over her belted waist. Her clothes were a depressing sludge brown and her skirt was droopy. But she was wearing patent-leather high-heeled sandals.

"May we come in?" asked Hamish as he and Charlie tucked their caps under their arms.

She suddenly looked ready to faint. "Is it Paul? Has anything happened?"

"No, no. Steady now," said Hamish. "We just cannae find him. We'll all go inside and Charlie here will make you a cup of tea."

She guided them into what she called "the lounge." It was a cold room. The fireplace had been blocked up and the hearth was filled with orange crepe paper. A set of bookshelves full of old leather-bound books took up one wall. The mantelpiece was covered in framed photographs of

Mrs. Walters at various stages of her life. Hamish noticed there were no photos of Paul. He explained about the last time Paul had been seen.

"Why are you asking me?" she demanded. "I barely knew the man."

"Well, *barely* seems to be the word for it. To put it crudely, you and Mr. English were seen shagging in the vestry."

Charlie came in and handed her a cup of hot sweet tea. She blindly took it from him and the cup rattled in the saucer as her hand shook.

She put the cup down on a small bamboo side table, folded her hands in her lap, and said, "We are engaged to be married. Paul swore me to secrecy. He said he couldn't bear gossip. But we never, ever did anything like that! I am a minister. Also, the vestry is locked. Where is he?"

"That is what we and the rest of the police force are trying to find out. When did you last see him? And why did you just say you barely knew the man in one breath and then say you were engaged in almost the next? When did you last hear from him?"

"That would be yesterday afternoon. He was furious about something but he wouldn't tell me what it was. And I said I barely knew him because I didn't really know what I was saying."

Hamish promised to let her know as soon as Paul English was found but he was beginning to wonder if they would ever find him. He and Charlie called on daughter Holly who swore her mother was a saint and never, ever would blackmail anyone and how could they speak ill of the dead and began to cry so hard that a neighbour who had been looking after her phoned Strathbane and complained so Hamish was told to submit a full report in triplicate explaining his behaviour.

* * *

But the opportunity didn't arise to question her any more, for Holly suddenly left for Norway without informing the Scottish police. The Norwegian police said that her mother's body had been found and the daughter had identified it. A Mrs. Merriweather who had been on the cruise with Maggie had offered to pay for the funeral. Hamish's friend at headquarters, Jimmy Anderson, turned up at the police station just after Hamish had heard the news.

"I tried to get permission to go out there but it was no go."

"Why?"

"Pour me a whisky and I'll tell you."

"It is only ten in the morning."

"So what?"

"Oh, well, it's your liver."

"I got to thinking. What if this Mrs. Merriweather is actually Maggie?"

"What did the Norwegian police say?"

"They e-mailed a photo of Mrs. Merriweather. She's a

bit wrinkly and droopy but there's no way she looks like Maggie. The captain made a statement saying he often couldn't tell them apart—one old woman looked much the same as another to him. Cheeky sod. Wait a bit. The evening afore Maggie went overboard, he said the pair were *pretending* to be each other. He said that was when he had a good look at them and burst out laughing. He said Maggie was trying to sound American and Mrs. Merriweather was trying to sound Scottish and they were making a pig's ear of it. Oh, well, here goes. Rummel, rummel roond the gums. Look out stomach, here it comes!"

"How did they know she had committed suicide?" asked Hamish. "I mean, what if she was pushed overboard?"

"Member of the crew saw her. She fell from the upper deck. Alarm called. Ship stopped, alarm bells rung, search and search until the rich passengers began to bitch that this wasnae what they paid for."

"I wish I could get a real search of that house of hers. But the daughter will…wait a bit. The daughter's over in Norway."

"Holly will scream police harassment even if I could get a search warrant. Gosh. This weather fair gives a man a thirst."

Jimmy held out his glass and beamed as Hamish absent-mindedly poured a large measure of whisky into it.

"Of course," said Hamish slowly, "if me and Charlie happened to be passing and heard what we thought was a cry for help, well, as good policemen, we'd break in, wouldn't we?"

"I never heard that," said Jimmy. "Man, this is the grand whisky. I can aye tell the good ones."

"It's Japanese," said Hamish. "An American tourist was over in Japan and brought it back and gave it to me."

Jimmy glared into the contents of his glass. Pride told him to pretend it was awful and pour it down the sink. Honesty prevailed. It was alcohol. So what?

* * *

After Jimmy had left, Hamish drove up to the Tommel Castle Hotel, taking Lugs with him. Sally, the poodle, was almost permanently with Charlie. He was about to descend the stairs to Charlie's apartment when he heard the voice of Colonel Halburton-Smythe, owner of the hotel, talking to Charlie, and backed away. It was an odd friendship, that of the usually snobbish colonel and Charlie Carter. But the colonel also fancied himself as a detective and Hamish knew that if he told Charlie about going to Holly Bates's home, then the colonel would insist on following.

"Looking for me?" asked a voice behind him. He swung round. His former fiancée, Priscilla Halburton-Smythe stood there, blonde and beautiful as ever, and as cold as ice, Hamish reminded himself. Her lack of any sexual warmth was what had made him terminate their engagement, and yet part of him still yearned for her.

"Do you think you can get your father out of there?"

asked Hamish. "I need Charlie for police business and you know your father will try to come as well."

"Well, hullo, Priscilla, how are you, up here for long?" mocked Priscilla. "Don't worry. Go and have a coffee with Mr. Johnson."

* * *

Mr. Johnson, the hotel manager, looked up as Hamish and Lugs walked into his office. "Avoiding Hercule Poirot again?" he asked.

"Something like that."

"Help yourself to coffee and tell me all about Granny Dinwiddy committing suicide."

Hamish collected a mug of coffee from the coffee machine along with a packet of biscuits. "Why are these damned things always hermetically sealed?" he complained, tearing open the packet with his teeth. Two biscuits shot out and landed on the floor where Lugs gulped them down. "What's with the airline-type biscuits?"

"They were going cheap and we put a packet in each room with their free coffee and tea. Try another, and here's a pair of scissors."

When Hamish had successfully opened the packet, he said, "I think she was a blackmailer. I think maybe Paul English who I know was being blackmailed by her got fed up and said he was going to the police—something like that. I mean, she must have had a stronger hold on him than merely getting under the minimum wage for him to pay for a cruise and a set of new clothes. But then she was floating around some fjord while he was being murdered. Of course, he might be alive and just have cleared off."

"No sign of him yet?"

"The trouble is no one wants him found and if someone murdered him, well, there are suspects like the old Highland and Islands phone book. He must have insulted hundreds of people. I'm beginning to think we'll never find him."

* * *

Penny and Abby Worhy were sisters and not very much alike. Both were in their early teens. Penny, a black-haired beauty, was thirteen and her sister, Abby, small and thin with pointed features like an elf, was twelve. They had a metal detector which belonged to their elder brother, Callum, who was at Edinburgh University. They had seen a documentary on television about people who had found treasure with their metal detectors. Penny had suggested they try the peat bog up on the moors outside Lochdubh.

It was half term; the day was sunny and warm and Abby said she was sure they would find something really good like a Viking sword. But Penny laughed at her and said she was only interested in gold and silver.

They settled down on the tussocky grass and heather at the edge of the bog to eat a picnic lunch. But Abby couldn't wait. "Let me go first, Penny," she begged.

"Okay," said Penny. "But make sure you're on safe ground."

But Abby knew the bog well and was soon moving from one safe little island to another as she swung the metal detector over the bog. She nearly fell in with excitement when the detector issued its shrill alarm. "I've got something!" Abby yelled.

Penny hurried to join her. "I never thought what we would do if the thing was down in the bog," she said gloomily. "How do we search without being dragged down?"

"I think it's safe," said Abby. "It's been dry for ever so long. Look!"

She put her hand down into the bog and showed a small handful of dry peat to her sister. "I brought the brass coal shovel," said Penny. "I'll lie on my stomach and you hold my feet just in case."

"I should be the one to look," muttered Abby. But she held her sister's ankles as Penny began to dig. The small brass shovel flashed in the sunlight and Penny was soon covered in clouds of peat dust. "I've found something." The shovel clinked against metal.

Overcome with excitement, Abby released her grip on her sister's ankles and crawled forward. "We'll both use our hands to scrape around it," said Penny. "Look, Abby. Those look like handcuffs. Let's..."

"*No!*" screamed Abby. "Get your phone. Call Hamish."

"What?"

"Don't you see? Thon missing man was wearing handcuffs!"

* * *

Hamish got the call on his phone and sent Mr. Johnson to fetch Charlie. "Did you have to bring that poodle?" complained Hamish.

"You've got Lugs."

"Lugs is a dog. That's a *thing*."

"No superior rank is going to stop me from punching your head, *sir*."

"Sorry, Charlie. But we'll drop the beasts at the police station first. Blair will be on the scene."

* * *

When they arrived at the peat bog, Blair was there along with Jimmy Anderson, Superintendent Daviot, various detectives, and a squad of policemen already combing the moorland for clues.

Blair lumbered up to them, his eyes gleaming with malice as he surveyed them. "You useless pair. Join the squad out on the moor and bag anything ye find."

"I think we would be more use talking to the suspects," said Hamish. "I was the one who stopped them from throwing him in the loch the night he disappeared."

"Aye, that's right," said Charlie.

"My, my!" jeered Blair. "It's alive! My God, the teuchters are thick enough on the mainland but when they're frae the isles, they're brain-dead."

Charlie took an enraged step forward but Hamish put a restraining hand on his arm and said, "Do be careful, Charlie, we both know the detective to be capable of murder."

Blair was clenching his fists in rage when the colonel's high precise voice could be heard saying, "Peter, a word with you, if you please."

"A'right," snarled Blair. "Do whit ye have tae do!"

Hamish and Charlie went off but it was too late for Blair. Peter was Daviot's first name and Daviot and his wife had been invited to dinner at the castle by the colonel and all because of, as Daviot knew very well, the colonel's close friendship with Charlie.

"I did not know in these politically correct days," said the colonel, "that policemen were allowed to indulge in ethnic slurs."

* * *

"So," said Charlie, "where do we start?"

"We'll go over to the forestry. The ones who were trying to throw him in the loch were all forestry workers. The trouble is they're all from Glasgow and it would take someone with local knowledge to know about the peat bog."

"Who were they?"

"Two brothers, John and Harry Noble. The others? Tim Rankin and Sam Meachin."

* * *

The forestry workers were at first sullen until they realised they were not going to be arrested for assault. They said Paul had mocked their accents and sneered at their city and so they had decided to teach him a lesson. As Glaswegians, they did not possess the highlander's talent for lying and so Hamish was forced to believe them when they all swore that after Hamish had appeared on the scene, they had all gone home. The only thing they got of use from them was that just before Paul had started sneering at them, he had made a phone call.

As they strolled back to where they had left the police Land Rover with the dogs at their heels, Hamish said, "Usually it's sex or money. What was the name of that wee girl who claimed Maisie had carnival knowledge?"

"Fairy McSporran."

"Do you know where she lives?"

"Aye, I wrote it down." Charlie fished in his pocket and drew out a small notebook. As he searched the pages, Hamish leaned against the sun-warmed side of the Land Rover and watched the sun slanting through the pines and suddenly wished it were all over.

"Here we are," said Charlie. "It's number five, Dunmore Road, that's up the brae a bit behind the kirk. What did this Paul do afore he came up here?"

"I checked it up. He was a bank manager in Stirling and retired last year. Stirling police say he was very unpopular as he delighted in refusing loans. He was all right for a time because Scottish people of a certain age don't like change but the new generation said, 'The hell wi' this,' and changed banks. The bank was the Scottish Independent. They were alarmed at the loss of customers. They gave him a golden goodbye and so he came up here to torment us all."

"So it could ha' been someone from Stirling."

"I doubt it," said Hamish. "It was chance that someone who hated him found him wandering along the road with his hands handcuffed behind his back."

* * *

It showed all the signs of being a Christian household, thought Hamish gloomily as he and Charlie sat side by side on a slippery chintz-covered sofa. In front of them was a coffee table with various religious magazines arranged neatly on it. The wallpaper was cream with brown Regency stripes which somehow seemed to turn the room into a cage.

Mrs. McSporran came in carrying a tray with two steaming mugs of coffee and a plate of shortbread. "I put the sugar and milk in for you," she said. Hamish liked his coffee black but there was something intimidating about Mrs. McSporran's glittering eyes and jerky movements. She sat down on a chair opposite them. She was wearing very thick glasses which caught the sun shining in the window so that it was hard to read her expression.

Charlie was reaching for a piece of shortbread when Mrs. McSporran said in a severe voice, "We will now say grace."

She began to recite Robert Burns's Selkirk Grace:

Some hae meat and canna eat,
Some wad eat that want it;
But we hae meat and we can eat,
And sae the Lord be thankit.

"You may have your coffee now. Why do you want to see Fairy?"

What on earth made this grim matron give her daughter a name like Fairy, thought Hamish. Aloud he said, "Your daughter claims to have seen Mrs. Maisie Walters and Mr. Paul English in a compromising position. And I assume Mrs. Walters is a widow?"

"Aye, her first husband died a while back, so I heard. But to get to Fairy. The puir wee thing. When the reverend came around and told me, I skelpt that wee lassie's backside and told her never to lie again."

Said Charlie, "Her description of the event did not sound like lying to me."

She had a weather-beaten red face but it almost turned white. "This has got to stop," she shouted. "Mrs. Walters says she will take us to court for slander."

Had Mrs. Walters been a poor woman, then the gossip would have festered and burnt, but she was a reverend and Cnothan was still old-fashioned in its pecking order and ministers were the top of the tree.

"We'll leave that for the moment," said Hamish soothingly. "Now, the late Mr. English…"

"He's deid!"

"Yes, his body was found in a peat bog."

Mrs. McSporran fell to her knees on the haircord carpet and raised her hands to the ceiling. "You have heard my prayer, O Lord, and you smote the wicked."

Hamish took the opportunity to eat a piece of shortbread, which was surprisingly good.

"I must say," he remarked in a conversational tone, "I've never, ever tasted better shortbread."

Mrs. McSporran got to her feet and beamed on him. "I'll make you up a box to take home."

"You look to me like a verra intelligent woman," said Hamish while inside his head a voice jeered that she really looked like a demented ferret. "Now, Mr. English prided himself on his honesty and I am afraid he insulted an awful lot of people."

"That he did." She resumed her chair and smoothed down her skirt with work-roughened hands. "When Mrs. Walters told us she was engaged to the man, we was struck all o' a heap. He said awful things to me and everybody. I don't want to talk about it."

"You needn't tell me what he said. But did you hear anybody threatening to kill him?"

"Oh, the whole o' Cnothan. But nobody really meant it."

"I may need to come back with a social worker to speak to Fairy."

"Oh, dinnae dae that! Social workers are baby snatchers."

"Let's leave it for the moment," said Hamish.

Before they left, she gave him a box of shortbread.

Hamish thanked her and said, "My friend Dick Fraser and his wife, Anka, have a bakery business ower in Braikie."

She clutched his arm. "Their baps are the best in Scotland. Can you get me the recipe?"

Hamish promised to try.

Outside, he said to Charlie, "I'll call Priscilla and see if she'll join us."

"Why?"

"It's half term. We might find Fairy playing somewhere and we can interview her if we've got a female here."

"She's not official."

"Aye, but if we turn up here wi' a social worker, they'll be fleeing to the hills with their bairns."

Priscilla's tones were not friendly in the slightest. "So you've remembered to say hullo when you've decided you need help?"

"Aw, come on, Priscilla. I'll take you to lunch?"

"In Cnothan? No thanks. Oh, look, I'll come over and bring a picnic basket. See you."

CHAPTER THREE

The secret of life is honesty and fair dealing. If you can fake that, you've got it made.

—Groucho Marx

The McSporrans lived in a neat little bungalow only a few yards from the church. They found Fairy. She was perched on the wall of the graveyard, staring openmouthed at Priscilla. "Are you a fillum star?" she asked.

"No, I'm a computer programmer. I would like to talk to you."

Fairy nipped down from the wall. She was a small ginger-haired child with green eyes.

"I waud talk to you, miss," she said. "But them's the polis and my ma says she'll beat the living daylights out o' me if I ever talk tae the polis again. And the minister says I'll burn in hell."

"Okay."

* * *

"This isnae right, Hamish," complained Charlie. "Whatever you say, it's chust not legal."

"I'll worry about it when the time comes."

"Anyway, why are they all so frightened o' the social workers?"

"It was over twenty years ago now but in Orkney the children were dragged screaming from their mothers. The charge was child abuse. Some rubbish about satanic beliefs. Well, by the time it was proved a load o' rubbish, the bairns had been pretty much traumatised."

"Fairy's certainly talking a lot," said Charlie. They could just make out the lilt of her voice as she talked to Priscilla. "Do you never get fed up with this policing business, Hamish?"

"From time to time," said Hamish cautiously. "Not thinking of leaving, are you?"

Charlie shrugged. "Where would I go? I joined the police because there's no work for me on the island. There's the fishing but there's no room for anyone else. But I miss it. It's the most beautiful place in the whole wide world."

Hamish's phone rang. It was Jimmy Anderson. "Guess what?"

"What?" said Hamish patiently.

"It isnae murder."

"What the hell is it? The wrath of God?"

"No foul play. English simply staggered into the peat bog and sank."

"He could have been marched there at gunpoint," said Hamish.

"Listen, laddie, if you want tae keep your job, keep your trap shut. Everyone here's happy. Case closed. Goddit?"

"I've got it," said Hamish. "What if…?" But Jimmy had rung off. Hamish told Charlie the news.

Charlie was just about to say something when Priscilla came in. She patted Fairy on the head and told her to run along.

"So what did you get?" asked Hamish.

"I think she's telling the truth, but she begged me not to say anything because the minister had called and her mother had given her a whipping for telling lies."

"It doesnae matter now," said Charlie. "Case closed. The man wasnae murdered. He just staggered into the peat bog."

"I don't like it," complained Hamish when they were enjoying their picnic. "A man as arrogant as English—remember, he was a bit drunk—wouldn't cross over the moors. He didn't know the land around here. He'd stomp down the middle of the road, defying me to come and get him."

Hamish took out his phone and called Jimmy. "Who did the autopsy?" asked Hamish.

"Karen Black. Usual chap's down wi' the norovirus."

"I want a look at that body," said Hamish. "I don't know this Karen Black."

"Well, get down to the procurator fiscal's fast because his mother's coming up."

"He's still got a mother? I thought he would have bored her to an early grave. Right, I'm off."

Charlie looked reluctant and Priscilla said it was time she packed to go back to London so Hamish said he could go on his own.

* * *

A brisk wind was blowing as he drove across the moors under the shadow of the great mountains of Sutherland. Then as he crested a hill, there lay before him the long straight road to Strathbane, the town that Hamish considered a blot on the beauty of the Highlands.

He drove directly to the mortuary beside the procurator fiscal's office. It had been described in the press as a disgrace but nothing had been done to modernise it. Families used to seeing mortuaries on television with scientific instruments all around usually left the Strathbane mortuary in shock. It looked like a derelict garage. The door wasn't even locked. He opened it and went in.

The body of the late Paul English was lying on a wooden table covered in a blanket. Hamish gently bared it. The peat had preserved it beautifully. The body was wrapped in a hospital gown. Hamish peeled it off and then turned the body over. He let out a hiss of surprise. At the back of the neck was a little roll of fat, and when he lifted it with one gloved finger there was a clear mark of a stab wound. He took out his iPad and photographed it from every angle.

He rearranged the body and went next door to the procurator fiscal's office. The procurator was away visiting relatives in Inverness and his secretary said she had no authority to start up a murder enquiry so Hamish told her he was about to charge her with perverting the course of justice and covering up a murder until she turned pale and picked up the phone.

* * *

George, Colonel Halburton-Smythe, was sitting on the terrace of his hotel accompanied by Charlie and Hamish's two dogs. "So, you really are thinking of quitting the force?" said George. "I mean, where would you go?"

"Anywhere in the Outer Hebrides. I'm miserable here. Too big, too clumsy, and I hate police work."

"You could stay here and…and…be the hotel policeman."

"That's grand of you, George, but I'd like to go home. I've saved a bit. Maybe manage to get a wee croft."

The little colonel began to feel miserable. Charlie Carter was his first real friend. Usually he barricaded himself with petty snobbery, always ashamed that his family background had been in trade. He had nourished hopes that his beautiful daughter would marry some lord or other, but now he wished with all his heart she would marry someone like Charlie.

Charlie's phone rang. He listened and then said, "I'm coming." He rang off and turned to George. "I'm sorry. That was Hamish. Paul English was murdered after all."

* * *

Hamish was in trouble. Blair was raging, trying to say he had stabbed the body himself, and only the intervention of Peter Daviot—who had just received a telephone call from his wife saying that dear Priscilla had asked that Hamish be given every help—had stopped the fuming Blair in his tracks.

Then Hamish had suggested that Paul might have phoned someone and that his mobile might still be down in the peat bog. If they took a strong metal detector, the ground being still dry, they might be able to locate it.

But when everything had been assembled and they were leaving headquarters, the weather of Sutherland had made one of its mercurial changes and heavy squally rain was blowing in from the west. By the time they got to the peat bog, it was once more a sodden, dangerous morass. Blair, beside himself with bad temper, jumped up and down in a rage. The ground gave way and he began to sink. By the time the fire brigade arrived to rescue him, he had cursed and sworn at having his head held above the bog by Hamish.

He was still cursing and raging about highland idiots who couldn't leave well alone when Charlie suddenly snapped.

"Oh, shut up, ye nasty wee man," he shouted. "I wish tae God we'd left ye!"

A triumphant grin crossed Blair's fat features. "I charge you, Charles Carter, with threatening the life of a superior officer. Get the cuffs on him, laddies."

Nobody moved. "I'm ordering ye," roared Blair.

"I didnae hear a thing," said Jimmy Anderson. "We'd best be getting back. I see the ambulance turned up as well." He went over and had a word with the paramedics. They came rushing over with a stretcher. Blair tried to fight them off but Jimmy said soothingly that the poor man's brain had been turned by the ordeal so he was strapped into a straitjacket. As he was carried off, he looked at Charlie with murder in his eyes and Hamish shuddered.

The finding of the body had not been released to the press and so headquarters were able to cover up their mistake. It was back to plodding work again.

To his distress, Charlie was chosen to interview the minister, Maisie Walters, Hamish having persuaded Jimmy that women always felt safe with Charlie and would often tell him things they would not tell anyone else.

At first, it looked as if she would have liked to have slammed the door in his face, but realising it might make her look guilty of something, she let him in. Charlie, in his quiet, lilting voice, told her about the murder of her fiancé. She clutched hold of the arm of a chair for support. Charlie helped her to sit down.

"I'll chust be making you a cup o' sweet tea. Stay there!"

When he returned with a cup of tea laced with whisky he had found in a cupboard, she drank it gratefully. "Do you want me to call anyone?" asked Charlie.

"No. It's the shock. Who would want to murder Paul?"

The truthful answer, thought Charlie, was just about

everyone, but he said gently, "That is what we must find out. How long had you been engaged?"

"Just the three weeks before he died. Paul was very religious. He prided honesty." Her eyes suddenly filled with tears and she said harshly, "The engagement was broken off. So there!"

"Why?"

"We didn't see eye-to-eye and God told me to send him away."

"We'll be looking into his background. I don't think, as I recall, he had been married afore."

"No, he was very attached to his mother. She was to live with us after we were married. But the poor soul is suffering from shock."

"Wouldn't that have been difficult for you?"

"It might have been but I told Paul she would need to respect the fact that I was the lady of the house and we'd get on grand."

"And he agreed?"

"Oh, yes."

First lie, thought Charlie. That was a lie.

"You are a very attractive and perceptive lady," said Charlie. "Were you ever married afore this?"

"Oh, yes. My husband was a manager on one of the oil rigs. Goodness, it was boom time. He made such a lot of money. But he died eight years ago of cancer. I had once wanted to be an actress because I have a good presence but I felt the call of God and took orders instead."

Felt the call of showing off in the pulpit to a captive audience, thought Charlie cynically.

"I don't want to distress you at this bad time, ma'am, but there is the question of the wee girl, Fairy, and what she said she saw."

"I've been hard on that lassie, but you see Paul was interested in the theatre, like me. We have the panto here at Christmas and some concerts, but we were going to put on Tennessee Williams, *The Rose Tattoo*. It's a steamy play and we were rehearsing. But the Kirk Session got to hear of it and said it was indecent. Can you believe such a thing! So of course we didn't go on with it but they made me feel so ashamed, I didn't want anyone to know we had even thought of it. I'm sorry I was rough on wee Fairy but it's hard when everyone expects you to be a saint."

"I will be having a word with Fairy's mother," said Charlie. "You don't need to describe the play. Just that the Kirk Session thought a concert with a lot of people getting parts would be better. Do they drop their drawers in *The Rose Tattoo*? Sorry to sound so vulgar."

"No, that bit really was the wee lassie's imagination."

Another lie, thought Charlie. She should know by now that all us highlanders have got PhDs in bullshit and you cannae bullshit the bullshitters.

"I won't be troubling you any mair the day," said Charlie.

"You can stay to tea if you would like." She gave him a coy smile.

"That's right kind of you but I got a murderer to find."

* * *

Charlie drove slowly back to Lochdubh. The rain had stopped and he opened the side window, breathing in the wind blowing the scent of the isles all the way from the west. Lochdubh had seemed a paradise when he had first been transferred from Strathbane. But now he could not understand how Hamish could remain so calm. Hamish's previous sidekicks had been lucky in that they were more interested in things other than police work: Dick with his passion for baking; Clarry the chef, now at the hotel; and Willie Lamont gone to the restaurant trade. The nastiness of Blair, the bullying, the sight of dead bodies did not seem to impinge on their souls.

He would have been surprised to know that worry about him had brought the colonel and Hamish together.

Summoned to the hotel, Hamish listened carefully to George's story about how Charlie longed to go back to South Uist. "I'm sure you'll try to stop him going," said George miserably, "but I think he would be happier out of the force."

Hamish and George were seated in a corner of the hotel lounge. The colonel looked impatiently at the tall lanky policeman wondering, for the umpteenth time, why Hamish had broken off his engagement to Priscilla.

"Actually," said Hamish slowly, "I am worried. I'd miss him sore but here's the problem." He told him about his fears concerning Blair.

"But I shall tell Peter Daviot!" said the colonel, appalled.

"Wouldn't work. Blair can crawl his way out of anything."

"I could give Charlie money for a croft but I fear he wouldn't take it," said the colonel.

"No, he would not. I know he's got a bit put by. Let me think."

Hamish switched on his iPad and looked for croft land for sale in South Uist. "Look, there's plots at Ardmore. Offers of thirty thousand pounds. He's a young man. Surely he could get a loan or a mortgage. I've got a fourth cousin, Geordie Struthers, in South Uist. I'll dig up his number and get him to meet Charlie and lure him to the croft land."

"I could always visit," said the colonel wistfully, and Hamish was sorry for him for the first time as he saw the loneliness peering out of his eyes.

Hamish felt sad at the thought of losing such an amiable policeman as Charlie. Strathbane would find—if Blair had anything to do with it—someone really horrible to replace him.

As the summer dragged on, Hamish thought of it as the plodding days. Charlie had promised to stay until the case was closed, but nothing seemed to break. One day Hamish managed to meet Blair's wife for a coffee. She listened carefully as he told her his fears about Blair. But she laughed them off for the simple reason that Mary did not want to know. Her marriage to the drunken detective had got her off the streets and she felt she knew how to manage him.

* * *

After Charlie had given Hamish his report that evening, Hamish said, "It does make me think our reverend might be a murderess. Maybe he told her the engagement was off. If she had been dropping her knickers for him and was not that sort of woman, she'd be thirsting for revenge. Anyway, I would like you to stay a bit and then me and George have a plan for you."

"Aye? What's that?"

"It's like this, Charlie, you've lost your taste for police work and I don't think you'll get it back. Me and George know of some croft land for sale in South Uist. You could get a mortgage or a loan. Put a caravan on it until you get a bit o' dosh. Few sheep. All set. There's a big trade in seaweed these days. You could try to get in on that. You got any folk there?"

"Not really. Most of the family left for America like I told you and there was just me. They had sold the house and croft so I was in digs and had to come here to make a bit o' money because there was nothing there. Mind you, I could have gone with them to America but I couldnae bear to be that far from the isles."

"Aye, well, I want to keep you away from Blair as much as possible. I think the drink is finally turning his brain."

"Hamish, when I leave, can I take Sally with me? You never really took to the wee poodle."

"Go ahead. Lugs seems happy enough when she's either

around or not around. Maybe neither of us got over losing Sonsie. Let's have a dram and drink to your future freedom and then let's go over this damn case. Oh, I hope it isnae someone from this village. He would be walking away with his hands handcuffed behind his back. He would make his way through the village. He would find somewhere to lie low so that he could be sober by the time we got him and say I was persecuting him."

Hamish brought down the bottle of whisky and poured two generous measures.

"It is chust a wee idea," said Charlie. "I mean, me, I cannae believe any woman would fancy a man like English. But the minister did. Maybe he had one on the side. Anyone in Lochdubh qualify?"

"There's a thought," said Hamish. "A man like English liked power over people. He must have been one hellish bank manager. Probably jerked off every time he turned down a loan."

Charlie blushed. "Sorry," said Hamish quickly, thinking how old-fashioned and easily shocked Charlie could be. "So who have we got?"

"I saw a wee lassie in Patel's the other day," said Charlie. "'Well, look at the size o' you!' she says, all flirty."

"Pretty?"

"Bit smelly. Greasy hair. Good figure."

"Smelly in this day and age?"

"She's staying at Mrs. Mackenzie's boardinghouse and madam only allows one bath a week so I cannae blame her for being a wee bit ripe. Also, Mrs. Mackenzie does her washing for her but on wet days hangs it up on the pulley in the kitchen so the clothes get to smell o' chips or mutton broth. I know that because some tourist complained about it when we were having a chat."

"What is her name and what does she do?"

"She's called Alison Ford and she's a nurse at Braikie hospital."

"So why not find digs in Braikie?"

"Says Lochdubh is cheaper."

"Wait a bit," said Hamish. "I cannae imagine such as Mrs. Mackenzie allowing any nookie under her sacred roof."

Charlie often amazed Hamish by his insight. "I think to a man like English," said Charlie, "power over someone would be more titillating than sex. Say he meets her in Braikie as if by chance, tells her about his engagement but is struck by her beauty and yaddy-yaddy."

"We've won out on far-fetched ideas before this," said Hamish. "Finish your drink and we'll chew some peppermints and see if we can see her."

* * *

But Mrs. Mackenzie told them that Alison was on the night shift. She finished at six in the morning.

"We'll get her when she comes out," said Hamish. "I could go alone but I want to keep an eye on you. I don't trust Blair."

* * *

Mary, Detective Chief Inspector Blair's wife, was a worried woman. She could normally handle her husband but he had started uttering threats against Charlie Carter, not his usual drunken rant, but with something vicious at the back of his piggy eyes. Hamish's fears began to haunt her.

So as Charlie and Hamish had an early night to prepare for the dawn drive to Braikie the next morning, Blair arrived home, cold and wet and in a beastly mood. He had managed to get himself released from hospital earlier that day. The rain was now blowing straight in from the Atlantic in gusty cold blasts.

He cursed and raved against Charlie and said he would see him in hell. He was drunk and his eyes gleamed with a wet look when he said, "But I hae the wee present for him." To Mary's horror he pulled a wash-leather pack out of his briefcase and produced a gun. "It's a Smith and Wesson .357 Magnum," said Blair proudly, "and bye-bye Charlie."

"You're going to commit murder!" shouted Mary.

He sobered quickly, wishing he had never shown her the gun. "Just pulling your leg, lassie," he said. "Found it lying by the side o' the road. I'll put it in the stockroom at headquarters tomorrow."

"Like a dram?" asked Mary. "I've got the fire in the lounge. Go through, pet, and put your slippers on."

Blair waddled off, dropping his wet coat and scarf on the floor for her to pick up. Mary went into the kitchen and poured a stiff measure of whisky. Then she went to the medicine cupboard and took out a sleeping draught hidden inside a vitamin supplement packet. She poured a generous measure into his drink. She had found the sleeping medicine to come in useful in the past when he had looked as if he was going to beat her up.

Blair was soon asleep, his mouth hanging open, snoring loudly. Mary opened the briefcase and gingerly took out the revolver. Then she phoned Mrs. Daviot. "It's me, Mary," she cooed. "I would be most awfully grateful if you could help me with a wee problem."

"Anything eh cehn do to help," said Mrs. Daviot in tones of strangulated gentility.

"My man's just come back from the hospital and he found a revolver just lying by the roadside and he thinks it's too late to get it to the stockroom at headquarters but I hate guns and…"

"Don't you worry, my pet. Eh'll get Peter to send an officer round right away."

CHAPTER FOUR

Seldom, very seldom, does complete truth belong to any human disclosure; seldom can it happen that something is not a little disguised and a little mistaken.

—Jane Austen

There are women who are beautiful and never realise it, and there are women who are not but who think they are absolutely gorgeous and irresistible to men. Alison Ford belonged to the latter category. As she mostly chased after the unobtainable, married doctors or surgeons, she could dream that they were dying with passion for her but frightened of their wives.

Hamish said they had a few questions to ask her and suggested they move inside to the hospital canteen because the morning, although sunny, was cold. To Hamish's disappointment, she did not seem in the least worried by their visit, and tripped ahead of them to the canteen, swaying her hips, which, in a girl only five feet tall, did not have the effect she thought it was having.

Charlie brought mugs of coffee and they settled down on plastic chairs at a plastic table.

"So what have my bad boys been up to?" she asked.

Seeing them puzzled, she laughed. "Oh, it's some of the old boys from the geriatric ward. Always wandering off. They're quite cunning, the way they manage to escape."

"No, Miss Ford," said Hamish solemnly. "It concerns your friendship with the late Paul English."

"Who?" she asked the ceiling.

"The man who has been found murdered in a peat bog."

"I didnae know him."

Charlie took a gamble. "Yes, you did, Miss Ford, and you should not lie to the police. He came to you the night he was killed."

She began to cry, or rather, to simulate crying, because when she finally removed her handkerchief from her eyes, they were dry.

"You can make a statement here or back at police headquarters," said Hamish.

"Okay," she said suddenly and harshly. "He phoned me, right? Said he needed help. He said to come down the fire escape to the garden at the back. I thought he looked funny handcuffed like that, but he hissed at me to get some cutters. I said I didnae have any and he called me a useless bitch. Me! He promised to ditch that minister frump and marry me. He did! I told him to take a hike."

"Quite the contortionist," said Hamish. "How did he manage to phone you with his hands handcuffed behind his back?"

"He must ha' phoned me from the pub afore you put them on. We sometimes meet in the wee garden at the foot o' the fire escape. He said a few more nasty things and went out onto the road and along the waterfront and that's the last I saw of him."

"What was his interest in Maisie Walters?" asked Hamish.

"Dunno. He wouldna talk about her."

"Grant me patience," muttered Hamish. "You say he told you he was prepared to ditch Mrs. Walters and marry you, right? He must have said something."

"Just that he was right tired o' her."

"Okay, I'll type this up and get you to sign it. Report to the police station tomorrow morning at nine o' clock."

* * *

"Let's go and call on Dick," said Hamish. "I could do wi' a decent cup of coffee."

Hamish always had to fight down a feeling of jealousy when he saw Dick's Polish wife, Anka. She was so glamorous, long-legged and auburn-haired, she was every man's dream and yet she had settled for small, round Dick Fraser.

Anka was busy with the accounts but Dick ushered them into his comfortable living room and served them bacon baps and strong coffee.

"So," said Dick, "yon Paul English was stabbed with maybe a sword."

"How the hell do ye know that?" exclaimed Hamish.

"Lady Campbell-Sythe dropped by for the baps. Her husband is the pathologist they got up from Glasgow fast after it turned out wee Karen Black didn't know an arse from an elbow. He says it looks like a flat blade that curved to a tip, like a claymore, some sort of broadsword."

Hamish groaned. "If I tell headquarters that, Blair will have us doing a house-to-house search in the village and anyone wi' any sense would ha' chucked the weapon down into the peat bog."

"He cannae have sunk that far into the peat bog," said Charlie. "I mean, it was the handcuffs that set off the metal detector. It was dry a bit before the rain came and then that long dry spell. Folk are always dumping stuff. Maybe there's an old car or something down there. Haven't they got sophisticated equipment for a proper search?"

As if in answer to his question, the phone rang. It was Jimmy. "You've to get yourself ower here," he said. "The bog."

"Right," said Hamish. He rang off and told them. "Wait a bit," said Dick. "I'll pack you a lunch."

"Anka's a lucky woman," said Charlie.

Hamish looked huffy but refrained from saying anything.

* * *

The wind had changed round to the east when they arrived at the bog. Hamish was relieved to see that Blair was not one of the party watching the excavation.

Jimmy joined them. "Where's your menagerie, Hamish?"

"The dogs? I left them back at the station."

"Funny that. When Sonsie was alive, you used to take the animals everywhere."

"Alive! What the hell do you mean?"

"Some yobs have been shooting on Ardnamurchan. They found a dead cat."

Hamish looked wildly around as if for escape. "Steady, lad," said Jimmy. "It's probably not yours. Settle down. It wasnae a wild cat. Someone's pet."

Hamish hunched his shoulders against the wind. If only English hadn't been such a rude womanising bastard. The Highlands were probably littered with folk dying to kill him. He longed to set off for Ardnamurchan but knew he would be in trouble if he did. Then what of English's life before he retired? He would enjoy humiliating people in desperate need of money.

"Anything on English's background in Stirling?" asked Hamish.

"Lots o' nasty stuff. Insulted hundreds."

"So why did he keep his job?"

"Like I said earlier, he didn't. Got the golden push last year. Before that, people kept a bit quiet about it, not wanting the neighbours to know they were in debt."

"Why isn't Blair here?"

"Got a drug bust. Besides, he's on the wagon. Different man entirely."

"They've got something," said Hamish. "Look, it's someone's old fridge. He must have landed on that, which is why he was so near the surface. Fancy a bite? Dick's packed a big lunch."

"Lead me to it," said Jimmy. "Ah, the grand days of Dick Fraser. We'd be on a stakeout and in seconds, Dick would have the table and chairs out and the stove on. Blair wants houses searched for swords, but it's daft. Have you been to an antiques fair or even a car boot sale? They're all displayed in the open, everything from scimitars to sabres. The old days in Glasgow, they used razors. Now it's swords. Man, is that chicken?"

Charlie said suddenly, "Has anyone talked to the Currie sisters?"

Hamish burst out laughing. "No one's feeling that masochistic, Charlie."

Charlie solemnly took another bite of chicken sandwich, a sip of coffee from one of Dick's thermos flasks, and said slowly, "They see a lot. They hear a lot. If I was to go down there and be nice and patient, I might just get something."

"Go on then," said Hamish. "You're a brave man. Take the Land Rover and come back for me as soon as you can."

* * *

Charlie bought a tin of shortbread from the gift shop at the hotel before going on into the village and knocking at the door of the Currie sisters' little cottage on the waterfront. Normally the sisters would have been offended at the gift as they considered they baked the best shortbread for miles around, but the tin had a romantic painting of Bonnie Prince Charlie bowing before Flora Macdonald, and the elderly twins became quite misty-eyed as they looked at it. Then Charlie was ushered into their overcrowded little parlour and plied with scones and tea. In a roundabout way, Charlie talked about his longing to get back to the isles and then said the present case had "fair sickened" him. He said he considered the ladies very noticing and perceptive. Had they, for example, heard or seen anything strange the night Paul English was killed?

Charlie had become expert at tuning out Jessie's chorus of what her sister had just said. He was made to swear on a large Bible that he would not reveal his source or the murderer's cohorts would come after them. The sisters watched a great deal of American television. A savage squall of rain hit the window and Charlie wished they would hurry up because Hamish must be getting a right soaking.

* * *

Hamish listened in amazement when Charlie, on his return, told him what the sisters had witnessed. Woken by the shouting outside the bar, they had put on their dressing gowns and gone outside to the garden gate. They saw the fuss die down and, as it was a mild night, were examining their flowers when suddenly they saw Paul stumbling along the waterfront. They had seen him go round the side of Mrs. Mackenzie's boardinghouse and then come out again. They hid in the bushes and he went past. Then his voice came faintly back to them, saying something like "Well, you took your time," and after that nothing.

"If only they would find that phone," said Hamish, when Charlie reported to him, "and if they do, let's hope they have the skill to get a number out of it. He must have phoned someone else before he was attacked in the pub."

Jimmy's phone rang. He listened, scowling, and when he had rung off, he said, "Bad business. One o' you had better get down to the village. A wee lad has tried to hang hisself in his father's garage."

"Which wee lad?" demanded Charlie.

"Johnny Derry."

"The one that was the menopause baby. Must be about eleven years old now. I'll go," volunteered Charlie. "I know the family."

"Maybe bullying," said Hamish. "He's a wee chap and his father is the physics teacher at his school. Check his mobile phone and his iPad. Social media be damned. Social murder."

* * *

The ambulance had left when Charlie arrived so he raced after it to Braikie hospital. A nurse at the desk on the children's ward told Charlie that the boy was all right, just a bruised neck.

A long corridor led to the children's ward. Charlie Carter turned that corner and fell very deeply in love.

At the end of the corridor was a six-foot-tall vision in a police uniform. Naturally golden hair was pulled back under a cap. Her face was a pale disk in front of Charlie's suddenly blurred eyes as he walked towards her as if in his sleep.

He took her hand in his and said, "Will you marry me?"

And she replied, "Oh, probably. You've come about the wee boy?"

Her eyes were pale grey with glints of silver and her soft voice sang of the isles.

"I am not in the way of falling in love," said Charlie. "Did the boy have a mobile?"

"Yes. Full of nasty messages calling him a wimp and saying he's gay and worse than that."

Her pale skin was delicately tinged with pink. "The parents are with him. I thought they were his grandparents."

"I'll be having a word with all the wee bastards at that school and I'll bring the fear of the law, hell, and damnation down on their feral heads," said Charlie, "and then what about dinner this evening?"

"I don't know. It depends how long they want me to stay with the boy, but Victim Support should be along soon."

"What brought on this persecution?"

"The wee lad had a girlfriend. She started texting him about a thousand times a day so he said he was dropping her."

Charlie walked into the ward.

* * *

Mr. Derry was sitting a little way away from the bed, his head in his hands. His wife was holding her son's hand. Both parents were grey-haired and in their fifties.

Charlie tapped the father on the shoulder and jerked his head to indicate the man should follow him outside. "How's the wee chap?" asked Charlie.

"He'll have a sore throat. Why didn't he tell us?"

"It's difficult. Will you be suing the lassie's family? What's her name?"

"Nessie Burns, and a damn wee Lolita if there ever was one."

"I would advise you to let the matter drop after I've put the fear of God into the lot o' them. The boy's still got to go to school and you've got to work there."

"I don't. Physics teachers are in demand. We can move."

"It might be healthier for the boy to see it through. I'm telling you, by the time I'm finished with them, your lad is going to be the most popular boy in the school."

* * *

When Charlie strode into the assembly hall of the Cnothan elementary school, Johnny Derry's classmates were standing with their parents. On a table lay a selection of mobile phones and iPads. Next term they would all be bussed into Strathbane High School.

Standing at the podium, Charlie glared at them all. "Murderers!" he shouted. "That's what you are. You can kill with words and you damn near did. Step forward, Nessie Burns."

A cheeky-faced moppet with hair tied up with tartan ribbons stepped forward followed by her father. "Does it make you proud to have nearly caused the death of a boy?" yelled Charlie. "You should be locked up!"

The father raised his fists. "Oh, come on, mate," said Charlie. "I'd love to arrest you. Now hear this. The father won't sue unless... *unless* this happens again. Geddit?"

A scrawny woman said, "Children are innocent creatures."

"Pah! This age? They are feral monsters. Now get your phones and bugger off and never, ever let this happen again."

Charlie strode out. He was determined to keep an eye on the boy. But his heart sang. Her name was Annie West and she was from South Uist. Like Charlie, she was beginning to hate the job. And, oh, blessed angels! The vision was having dinner with him that very evening.

* * *

Hamish was chilled to the bone and wondered what had happened to the summer when he arrived back at the police station that evening. He got out of his uniform and hung it up to dry. Then he had a hot shower and put on old clothes, wondering where that phone of English's could be. Probably down another bog. It seemed as if everything anyone wanted rid of had come out of that bog—fridge, cooker, skeleton of a cow, two dogs—but no phone or sword.

He noticed that Sally was missing and assumed the little poodle was up at the castle with Charlie. Lugs didn't seem to mind. It was almost as if the odd dog with the blue eyes was happy to have his master all to himself.

As he walked into his living room, he realised it was bathed in a golden glow. He went back out and opened the kitchen door. The evenings never get dark in the summer in the far north of Scotland.

The sun was turning the loch into molten gold. All the black clouds had rolled away and the air was sweet and fresh: full of the smells of tar, seaweed, wild thyme, and the pine forests on the other side of the loch.

He stood there for a long time, a half smile on his face, when all at once he felt menace coming from somewhere. His thoughts flew to Blair. He went indoors and fried up two slices of haggis and a couple of eggs and tomatoes for his supper. He then cooked some deer's liver for Lugs.

He could not believe in such a miracle change in Blair, as reported by Jimmy. He still felt uneasy when he had finished eating so he walked back out to the waterfront. Then he saw Blair. He was peering through the windows of the Italian restaurant, a brooding look of malice on his face. Blair turned and saw him and went rapidly to his car, jumped in, and drove off.

Hamish opened the door of the restaurant and walked in. Charlie and Annie were at a corner table, so wrapped up in each other they weren't even aware of his approach.

"Charlie," said Hamish sharply, "Blair's haunting you. He was outside the window a few moments ago, looking like the first murderer. His wife says he's off the booze and behaving like a lamb, but I can't believe it."

"Want to join us?" asked Annie.

"No, I've just eaten. Do be careful, Charlie."

"Jimmy was trying to get you earlier. He's up at the bog. They've found a phone."

"Is Jimmy still up there?"

"He's thirstily heading for your kitchen."

Hamish hurried back to the police station in time to meet Jimmy. "I've heard about the phone," he said.

"It's gone down to Glasgow by special courier to some expert. Maybe we'll get a break at last. What about a wee dram?"

"Wee it'll have to be. Come ben. I'm worried about Blair."

"Why? He's off the booze. Behaving like an angel. Talk o' the station."

"I don't believe it," said Hamish. "Yon scunner must be on something. I saw him watching Charlie through the restaurant window this evening and he looked evil."

"A bit mair whisky, man! That's an eyedropperful. Better. Cheers. Rumour has it that Charlie has fallen for big Annie from the isles. Stands to reason. She's like a female Charlie."

"Could Blair be on some sort of drug?"

"Get that wife o' his to search. She's a pal o' yours."

Jimmy's phone rang. He listened and when he had rung off, he said, "Summoned by Blair. Both of us wanted at headquarters."

Hamish was following Jimmy out of the village when he suddenly screeched to a halt and sounded the horn. Jimmy stopped, got out, and came back, saying, "What's up?"

"That," said Hamish, pointing.

"That" was a classic scarlet phone box.

"So what?" demanded Jimmy. "His hands were handcuffed behind his back."

"His nose wasn't," said Hamish. "Or he could have got a pen out of his breast pocket with his teeth. Jimmy, please get them to dust it in the morning. The locals all have smartphones now but the tourists like it."

* * *

Charlie was emerging from the restaurant, his arm around Annie's shoulders, when a sneering voice stopped him in his tracks. "My, if it isnae Sir Galahad hisself wi' the office bicycle."

Blair confronted them, a fat grin on his face. Charlie looked him up and down and then before Blair could move, Charlie pinioned his arms by his side, carried him easily down the steps to the loch, waded in, and ducked the raging detective under the water.

When Blair emerged spluttering, Charlie said, "That should clean your dirty mouth out."

Charlie was strolling back to join Annie when Blair shouted, "Turn around!"

Turning slowly round, Charlie found himself looking into the barrel of a revolver. The fact that the revolver was wet didn't help because he knew most modern guns can fire underwater.

"You're toast," jeered Blair. "You and that whore. As far as I'm concerned, all you teuchters should be dropped in the Minch. I'm defending myself, see? You assaulted your superior officer. I just happened to find this revolver up on the moors and I felt obliged to shoot you right in the balls. Am I loving this!"

He pulled the trigger. Charlie leapt to the side and the bullet whizzed harmlessly past him. Mad with rage, Blair raised the gun to fire again when the little poodle Sally sank her small sharp teeth into his ankle. He kicked the poodle savagely away but it returned and bit him again. He turned to bring the butt of the gun down on the dog's head but Charlie dived for his legs and sent him flying back into the loch. Annie ran down and into the loch. She was wearing a long white chiffon dress. The locals who were now crowding the waterfront said later she looked like one of them Greek goddesses. She bent down and felt underwater. Blair let out an animal scream of pain. Then she held up the revolver and handed it to Charlie just as Hamish came driving up, siren going and lights flashing.

Jimmy Anderson followed behind. "He attacked me. I had tae defend maself," shouted Blair.

"Excuse me," said a dapper little man, joining them. "I am Joseph White, lawyer, on holiday and I heard that officer insult ethnic minorities, threaten the tall policeman with a gun, and insult the lady by calling her a whore and the office bicycle. A number of us have recorded it on our phones as evidence."

"Detective Chief Inspector Blair," said Jimmy, "you are under arrest."

"Piss off!" roared Blair.

Charlie swung him round and handcuffed him while Jimmy read out the caution.

* * *

"Well," said Jimmy later when they were seated in a pub near police headquarters, "who'd have thought he'd go that far? Maybe he murdered Paul English. Wouldn't that be lovely? He's out on his ear now. He cannae wiggle out o' this one. But did you see Annie when her dress was wet? Man, that's the sort you slay dragons for."

"Stop drooling. Charlie's coming back wi' the drinks."

"I've been thinking," said Charlie, "the enquiry starts tomorrow with all the bloody forms in triplicate and it's going to go on for days. I'm suspended from duty and so is Annie."

"So you both go to the doctor," said Hamish, "and claim

you are suffering from post-traumatic stress and need at least a week away from bureaucracy. Where's Annie now?"

"Just walked in the door." All the men got to their feet. She had changed back into uniform and her hair was pushed up under her cap.

"Oh, no," groaned Hamish. "You're too healthy. Take her away, Charlie, and show her what tae do. What is it, Jimmy?"

Jimmy had just rung off and was signalling for Charlie and Annie to wait. "That was the big boss," he said. "He wants to see the pair of you."

"Okay," said Hamish. "Annie, get back into that white dress and muss up your hair and cling to Charlie like a broken reed."

Jimmy snorted. "Broken reed. You've been reading *The People's Friend* again." *People's Friend* specialises in romantic stories and as it is about the last magazine to do so, it sells all over the world.

* * *

Daviot looked in dismay at what appeared to be the wreck of Annie West. His wife had just been on the phone, demanding that Blair get the sack, but Daviot feared Blair still held on to some compromising photos of his wife and reminded her of her past folly to shut her up.

Daviot rang the buzzer on his desk and his secretary, Helen, came in. "Helen, my dear," said Daviot, "you remember when Superintendent McTavish visited from Glasgow, he gave us a bottle of Drambuie?"

"He gave *me* a bottle, yes," said Helen.

"I think we could all do with a wee dram and I saw you still had it and…oh…bring it in and buy yourself another on the road home, and some nibbly bits."

The efficient Helen was soon back with glasses, Drambuie, and biscuits and cheese. "Strong smell of onion in here," she said nastily as she left.

A pure crystal tear rolled down Annie's white cheek.

"Oh, my dear girl, you must not cry," said Daviot. "I heard when you were on your way here that you are both suffering from post-traumatic stress so I would like you both to take at the very least a week off. Now, Constable West, drink that down."

Annie blinked at the size of the measure, guessed that Daviot somehow did not know that Drambuie was a liqueur whisky, and knocked it back.

"Good girl," beamed Daviot. "Have another. Help yourself, Carter. Now, we all know that poor Mr. Blair has suffered a severe nervous breakdown."

"I am sure he will soon recover in retirement," said Charlie.

"Perhaps. But he is a good officer with many years of experience. Let us see how it goes. This is a very smooth drink. Have another."

* * *

Later that evening Jimmy and Hamish were seated in Mary Blair's flat examining a bottle of pills.

"I found these under the mattress," said Mary. "Oh, God, is this what caused him to flip his lid? I'm worried sick they'll take his job away and I'll be stuck with him all day."

"Where is he at the moment?" asked Hamish.

"He's in Raigmore Hospital in Inverness."

"There isn't a possibility that it was Blair who killed English?" said Hamish.

"I think I would have heard him muttering and threatening."

"We'll get these analysed," said Jimmy, putting the pills in a forensic bag.

* * *

Hamish dropped Jimmy off at headquarters. "You cannae be hoping for much from that phone box," he said, "if English used a pencil."

"I've got a geek checking with the phone company on calls made that night from that box and to where and what time."

Jimmy wished he'd thought of something so obvious and became angry. "Ye should have told me, Hamish. Stop trying to do my job. Anyway, numpty, ye have tae put money in a phone box."

"Not if you dial 999," said Hamish and drove off.

* * *

A week later summer returned to Sutherland, turning it into a blue county. The soaring mountains captured the soft blue of the sky, and out on the Atlantic the blue men that the old people still believed in rode the huge waves. Annie and Charlie had gone to South Uist to look for a piece of croft land. They had called on Hamish before they had left. Annie said she had a good bit of money put by and Charlie shouldn't care about using it as she planned for him to do all the work. They were to be married in Lochdubh and Hamish was delighted to be asked to be best man.

Hamish stood on the waterfront, taking in deep breaths of crystal-clear air. Charlie and Annie had taken the poodle with them. His mobile phone rang and the glory of the days fell from his shoulders as he sensed he was not going to like what he was about to hear.

It was Jimmy. "Get the drinks ready, laddie. Open the champers. I come with great news."

"What…?" But Jimmy had rung off.

Hamish bent down and patted Lugs. "I still feel it's going to be something nasty," he said to the dog.

But he sat down on the sun-warmed wall and waited until he saw Jimmy's battered old Ford crossing the humpbacked bridge.

Jimmy practically danced out of his car and handed Hamish a bottle of twelve-year-old Glenlivet.

"What's happened, Jimmy?"

"You will now address me as Detective Chief Superintendent James Anderson. Let's get some glasses."

"You've got Blair's job! He's finally got sacked?"

"Better than that. He's been arrested for the murder of Paul English. Didn't your geek find a call to headquarters?"

"My geek took off on holiday without telling me."

"Let's go ben. I've a raging thirst on me."

* * *

Seated in the kitchen, Jimmy poured two large measures, drained his and poured another, and beamed at Hamish. "I will tell you all. English does dial 999, one assumed with a pencil or his pointy nose. Emergency asks the problem. He says he has a complaint against one Hamish Macbeth who has abused his position as an officer of the law and if they don't send someone asap to get him out of the handcuffs, he will phone the press. Decide to send a young copper over and he's about to go when Blair comes in off a drugs raid and, always nosy, says, 'Where are you off to?' Hearing that one Macbeth might be getting into trouble, he offers to go.

"Now he says, when he got there, there was no sign of Paul nor did he hear anyone shouting for help. He looked up and down the road. No one. Why hadn't he contacted Macbeth? Said he was fed up with the whole thing and went back home to bed."

"Not enough to arrest him," said Hamish, looking puzzled.

"But we wondered why he had kept so quiet about it so we got a search warrant for his flat and guess what we found?"

Hamish stared at him and then said, "You found a sword. And it had English's blood on it. Where?"

"Under the mattress."

"But you found pills there! Why did this sword suddenly appear?"

"Don't spoil things. He must ha' been moving it here and there."

"Jimmy, what was in those pills?"

"It's a new nasty sort of amphetamine that ISIS have been feeding their followers. It makes people feel like Superman and without conscience or fear. Blair is desperate when he's off the booze so he hears about this in one of those dens of iniquity he occasionally drinks in. He's had it this time and will haunt you no more. He's in the cells, charged with murder, and his case comes up in the High Court in November. And you know the biggest laugh of all? He wants you to go and visit him."

Hamish looked distracted. "I'll do that now," he said.

"Well, what a party pooper you are," said Jimmy, putting the top back on the bottle. "I'm off."

* * *

After Jimmy had left, Hamish sat for a long time. If he just accepted that Blair was a murderer, he would be sent away for at least fifteen years. Fifteen years of peace and quiet! But that would mean leaving some murderer roaming Hamish's patch of heaven and he could not bear that. He was sure that Blair really had made the journey to see if he could make life difficult for one Hamish Macbeth and, having found no one there, had just gone home.

At last he went out and lifted Lugs into the Land Rover. As he walked around to get into the driver's seat, a hoodie crow strolled past, like a university don in a black gown, and threw him an age-old prehistoric look. Hamish shuddered and flapped his arms but the bird only shuffled a little bit away. Charlie would just shrug and say it was someone who had come back. But Charlie believed all sorts of weird things. And he had somehow found storybook love, pure romance.

That famous Scottish singer Kenneth McKellar had found it in his Swiss wife. Hamish had viewed photos of him singing Handel's "Silent Worship" to his wife and at one point, her face became beautified by sheer love. And yet, last heard, there was no plaque to the man that Sir Adrian Boult called the finest Handel singer of the twentieth century.

The Scots preferred Hollywood interpretations of their history, even putting up a statue to William Wallace, not as he really was, a knight who fought in full armour, but as Mel Gibson all kilt and woad.

Hamish felt that that sort of love was waiting for him, just around the corner. When he was with Priscilla, the old ache was there that somehow her chilliness would melt. And when he was in bed with Elspeth Grant, everything was as good as it gets except in the morning she was up and off, frightened her precious job might melt away.

The day was so fine, he suddenly did not want to spoil it by visiting Blair and set out for Ardnamurchan, hoping for a glimpse of Sonsie. To his dismay, he was stopped several times by rangers telling him that some gang in Glasgow were promising hunters game on Ardnamurchan shooting wild cats.

Hamish had bought a pound of venison sausages and a dozen eggs along with a packet of baps and a block of butter. Lugs sat and watched eagerly as Hamish lit the old Primus stove and put the pan of food on top to cook. Sonsie used to love sausages, he thought wistfully. After he had eaten, he fed some to Lugs and then put three on a dish on the ground a little bit away and whistled, the special whistle he had always used in the past to summon the cat.

Nothing happened. The sun beat down. Hamish sat in the shade of the Land Rover and soon was asleep.

The nights were still light, darkness being replaced by gloaming. A crack of gunshot and a screaming yowl jerked Hamish from his heavy sleep. Lugs let out a bark. A wild cat, blood pouring from its side, staggered into the road and fell down.

Sonsie!

Hamish made up his mind. Whoever had done this could wait. He must try to save Sonsie's life. That meant getting the cat back to Lochdubh because anywhere nearer they would simply take her away.

With feverish fingers, he prised open the lid of the medical kit. He injected the cat with morphine and put her on a saline drip after he had bound up the wound. Then he sped out of Ardnamurchan and as soon as he hit the road, he put on the siren and the blue lights.

A crowd of villagers gathered outside the police station. They watched as Dr. Brodie rushed in with his medical bag, followed later by the vet, Peter Abraham. "Sonsie," the crowd whispered. Mr. Patel came out with candles and the villagers started a vigil, Mr. Wellington at one point leading them in prayer.

At four in the morning, a gold disk of sun rose over the pine trees on the far shore and the birds began to sing.

At last Angela Brodie came hurrying along with a hospital trolley. Slowly the police station door finally opened and the cat with tubes attached to it was solemnly wheeled up the road to the vet's surgery, the candles flickering in the dawn breeze. Someone started a weird high-pitched highland Gaelic lament, and Hamish gave a superstitious shiver and began to pray as he had never prayed before. The villagers had covered up the fact that Hamish kept a wild cat before and they were determined no one should find out that Sonsie was back again.

The younger members often laughed at the old ones for their belief that people came back as seals, but deep in all their superstitious souls was the feeling that Sonsie used to be someone, someone special. Hamish was only vaguely aware that George, Colonel Halburton-Smythe, had joined the watchers.

The colonel was lonely without Charlie. Because his fortune had come from his father's shops, he had become a snob. He had married into the untitled aristocracy, but always he could feel that everyone knew of his common background. He could not sleep that night and saw his manager about to leave the hotel to join the vigil and, hearing about it, suddenly decided to go as well. That's what Charlie would have done.

Outside the surgery, after the cat had been wheeled inside, Mrs. Wellington boomed out that Mr. Patel would supply tea and breakfast at the church hall, everybody welcome. And somehow the colonel became part of it all, drinking tea, eating bacon baps, and listening to the soft voices of the villagers, feeling part of something at last.

* * *

When Hamish emerged, Angela Brodie went up to him and hugged his lanky figure. "Come home with me," she said.

"How is she?" asked Archie Maclean.

"Awfy bad," mumbled Hamish, and a long sigh went from mouth to mouth, like the wind crossing a wheat field.

* * *

Hamish was drinking tea laced with whisky when the doctor came in. "You've one bit of luck, Hamish," he said. "They used a rifle and not a shotgun. A shotgun would have blasted Sonsie out of this world. She's a rare big cat. If the rangers were out, they'll wonder what you were doing running away from the sound of a shot. We just have to hope they didn't see you take the cat."

"They didn't. I'll say I was chasing the men but the fact is I thought if I didn't get some help quick for Sonsie, she'd die."

"Go home to bed, man. There's nothing more you can do."

* * *

The next day, as the cat seemed to hover between life and death, Hamish decided to visit Blair. Jimmy had phoned and said Blair was still demanding to see him.

CHAPTER FIVE

There's one way to find out if a man is honest: ask him; if he says yes, you know he's crooked.

—Mark Twain

Hamish headed for police headquarters, Jimmy having explained that the detective had been transferred from the hospital to a police cell. He felt weary after the worry and the long night's vigil. He expected Blair to be ranting and raving, but it was a subdued man he almost didn't recognise who rose to greet him when Hamish was ushered into the cell.

Usually Blair was flushed and florid but his time off the booze had thinned his face and brought back some of its natural colour. "You've got tae help me, Macbeth," he said.

"That's what's puzzling me," said Hamish. "Why me?"

"Because you know I didnae do it. The rest are glad it's all sewn up and me with it. Aye. *Sewn up* is the word because

Daviot's getting a psychiatrist to say I'm off ma trolley so I'll soon be in a straitjacket."

"Okay. But I want your promise that in the future, you will do nothing to harm me."

"You got it. I'll even put it in writing."

"Right. Let's go back to the beginning. You find out English has complained about me and you see a way of me getting it in the neck so you rush over to Lochdubh. Go on from there."

"The phone box is empty. I'm right puzzled because he'd said on the phone you'd put the cuffs on him. I hadnae passed a soul on the road. Then I thocht that the bastard had phoned a pal and gone off, like, so I went hame."

"So now we come to the sword. Someone would have to have got into your apartment to put it there. Any sign of forced entry?"

Blair shook his head like a bull being tormented by flies.

"Think, man. Did Mary have any odd callers? Strange postman? Anyone she would let inside the house?"

"God knows I've asked her and asked her," said Blair.

"I think I'll have a word wi' her," said Hamish. "You were on drugs. Right?"

"Aye, and I'll stick tae whisky in future. They drive you daft."

* * *

Mary Blair had been crying and she had a black-and-blue bruise on one cheek. "Did he do that?" asked Hamish.

And when she nodded, he said furiously, "Och, why do we bother wi' the auld bastard. Let him rot in prison and give us all peace and quiet."

"But Hamish," wailed Mary. "I'd be the wife of a murderer. He never saved a penny. I'd be back on the streets. I tried to talk to Mrs. Daviot but she let out a squawk and hung up on me."

"Okay. Was there anyone in the house? Anyone collecting for something?"

"Some biddy from cancer research. But she wasn't inside the house. I had a couple o' pounds in my pocket and I put those in her collection box."

"Anyone else? Think!"

"The usual. Like the man to read the electric meter."

"What did he look like?"

"Small. Blue overalls. Thick wee glasses. Grey hair."

"Voice?"

"He didnae speak. Just took a note, nodded his head, and made for the door."

"Where is the electric meter?"

"In the bedroom."

"In the…! Mary. He could be fake. He could ha' slipped that sword under the mattress. This was after they had found your man's funny drugs? So why did the police come back?"

"Some phone call. A woman. Couldnae be traced."

"But you didn't leave him alone? The electricity man."

"Just to answer the door to the cancer research woman."

Hamish groaned. "Don't you see? Two of them could ha' been in cahoots. He's in the bedroom, she rings the bell. Takes a moment to slide that sword under the mattress.

"So. When forensics came to do the search, who was the main guy?"

"Don't know their names. But Jimmy Anderson should know."

"I didn't know he was actually here for the search."

"Aye, and a bit heartless he was. Kept saying I should be grateful to him for getting the old bastard banged up."

Hamish sat frowning. Jimmy had long coveted Blair's job. Jimmy hated Blair.

Hamish told her he would be back and went to the forensic lab. As usual, they all looked hungover, there having been a shinty game the night before. Their team had lost and they had consoled themselves with large quantities of cider.

Hamish asked if the result of the blood test on the sword had come through. "Oh. Yeah," said a skinny, geeky-looking fellow in a white coat. "Pig's blood. Always knew Blair had a good bit o' the pig in him, haw, haw, haw."

Hamish stood, puzzled. Either the setting up of Blair for the murder was a malicious prank, or the real murderer was a panicked amateur.

He slowly left the forensic laboratory and went in search of Jimmy. "Heard the news?" asked Hamish.

"Aye, but Blair's not off the hook. Questions still being asked. Why didn't he report he had been there and so on? And about being on that wonky drug. The deal seems to be he's heading back for the rehab for six weeks minimum. Oh, well, I'll just need to be grateful for small mercies."

"Why has that horrible man still got his job?"

"He crawls. He's got it down tae a fine art. He should set up classes for crawling."

"If only we could find his phone," said Hamish. "I mean English. He made a call from the pub to someone else. What about his fiancée? The minister?"

"Nothing there. We checked."

* * *

Hamish drove slowly back to Lochdubh. Summer had returned to the Highlands. When he got to the police station, he found Charlie and Annie waiting for him accompanied by the poodle, Sally. He took one look at their radiant faces and said, "When's the great day going to be?"

"Getting wed as soon as we can, and we've got a tidy wee bit o' croft land in South Uist. Going to raise sheep. We've got a big caravan and a surprise for George."

"What's that?"

"We got a wee baby caravan for practically nothing. If George gets lonely, he can help on the croft. How's Sonsie?"

"Still somewhere between life and death. You can come to the games at Strathbiggie on Saturday. I've got to raise money to pay the vet and there's a good prize for the hill run. Cheer me on. Come ben and have a coffee and I'll tell ye all about Blair."

Over cups of coffee, Hamish told them about the planting of the sword and the pig's blood.

"We've only got two more weeks before we finish with the police for good," said Charlie.

"I'll heave a sigh of relief when you're gone. If Blair gets back on the drug or even the booze, I wouldn't put it past him to come after you."

"Well, we'll be on Uist by the time he gets out o' rehab," said Charlie cheerfully. "Och, Hamish, why don't you chuck it all in as well? I mean, who cares about a scunner like Paul English. He's insulted most of the Highlands, and anyone could have done it."

"I don't like the idea of a murderer on my patch," said Hamish. "Once they start, they often go on."

He walked out of the police station with them when they left. How simple love was if you were lucky enough to find the right woman, thought Hamish, watching the glow on Charlie's face as he helped tall Annie into his car as if she were a fragile piece of china.

He then visited the vet where Sonsie lay with tubes sprouting out of her body. Her eyes were closed. "She's still in a coma," said Peter Abraham. "You have to face up to it, Hamish. If she doesn't come out of it soon, it would be better just to pull the plug."

"A bit longer," said Hamish. "I'm trying for the hill run prize so I'll be able to pay you."

"Aye, the news is round the village and they're all going to be there to cheer you on. Good luck."

* * *

Elspeth Grant arrived on Saturday to find the police station closed and the village largely deserted. Only Archie Maclean was there at the harbour to take a boatload of tourists round the loch as he augmented his fishing with tourism during the summer. He told Elspeth that Hamish had gone to try for the hill run prize so he would be able to pay the vet for Sonsie's care. Elspeth often thought Hamish's devotion to the cat bordered on the unhealthy but curiously, she asked the vet if she could see Sonsie.

"He'll need to make up his mind soon to end it," said Peter.

"Funny thing," said Elspeth. "You would sometimes think Hamish was married to that cat. Is Hamish sure it is Sonsie?"

"Sure as anything. Oh, there's the door. Let yourself out."

Elspeth turned for a last look at the large wild cat. And as she looked, one slit of eye opened and shone with yellow malice.

"Peter!" shouted Elspeth. "The cat's awake!"

The vet came running in. He bent over Sonsie and examined her. "No, it must have been a trick of the light," he said, straightening up. "No change at all."

But Elspeth felt a superstitious frisson as she got in her car and headed for Strathbiggie.

* * *

Most of the village had turned out, even the Currie sisters. The prize was one thousand pounds and attracted runners from all over Britain. It was more like mountain running, being in part up the steep flanks of Ben Corm to near the summit. Most of the runners were defeated by this, being used to flat marathons.

Hamish felt uneasy and wished he had trained for the run. Usually he made sure he was in peak condition. The weather could not have been better: sunshine and not a breath of wind. The heather was turning purple. The air was full of smells of candy floss, hot dogs, and car exhaust, and loud with noise from the usual fairground set up by the Gypsies.

The gun was fired and they set off. Hamish realised dismally that he was not going to win. And then, standing up on a rise, he saw Elspeth holding a placard which said, CAT WOKE UP.

Suddenly it seemed as if his legs had become like steel springs. He raced up the mountain as if jet-propelled followed by the hysterical cheers of the Lochdubh villagers. Then their noise faded and he seemed alone as he flew up over the mountain, plunging down the other side.

Then back came the roar of the crowd and the finishing tape bright in front of him as he crashed through it and fell on the ground, his heart pumping. Elspeth heard someone say, "He ran like a man possessed," and again felt that odd superstitious shudder. And who was that girl trying to wind herself around Hamish as he was led up to the judges' table?

"Get off, Alison," Hamish was saying.

"All that money," cooed Alison Ford, putting on her best seductive pout. "You come along tonight and I'll tell you something to solve yon murder."

"And I'll book you right now for withholding evidence," said Hamish.

"I'll deny the lot. Come along at eight o'clock and bring the champagne."

"Mr. Macbeth!" barked one of the judges. "We're waiting."

Hamish accepted the prize money, held up the trophy, and then looked around for Alison Ford, but the nurse had disappeared. Probably just lying again, he thought. But she had seen Paul on the night he disappeared.

Elspeth appeared at his elbow. "Well done, Hamish."

Hamish suddenly sank down onto the ground and put his head between his knees. "Feel a bit faint," he mumbled. "Be all right in a minute. What's this about Sonsie?"

"When I was there, she opened one eye. The vet said I must have imagined it but I'm sure I didn't. Let's get you back to the station and you can have a rest."

* * *

When Elspeth had made sure Hamish was tucked up in bed with Lugs beside him, she returned to the Tommel Castle Hotel in time to meet Charlie and Annie. She congratulated them on their engagement and admired Annie's ring of gold and garnets. She said she was surprised they hadn't gone to give Hamish a cheer.

"We got there too late," said Annie. "Headquarters is giving an engagement party for us tomorrow at three in the afternoon. Will you be able to come?"

Elspeth felt that old superstitious fear. She felt she should hurry back to Glasgow and forget about Hamish and wild cats that did not look like Sonsie. But she nodded. "I'll drop in. Then I'd better get off to Glasgow."

* * *

Although not specifically invited, the villagers of Lochdubh hired a bus to take the old ones to the engagement party, the others following by car. Mild sunshine tamed the usually savage countryside, and the flanks of the tall mountains were purple with heather. Some of the villagers were clutching presents out of the "Hamish Macbeth cupboard," having taken back presents when Hamish's engagements had failed. None of them believed in what they thought was a mercenary idea of giving a store list and so it looked as if Charlie and Annie would have at least five crystal jam dishes and four toasters.

The first person Hamish saw was Detective Chief Inspector Blair. He had thinned down and his normally groggy face was pale and his eyes clear. Really off the booze for once, thought Hamish. Trays of whisky were being carried around. Then the door opened and Charlie and Annie walked in.

They were in civilian clothes. Annie had her fair hair tied in a loose knot on top of her head. Her large grey eyes looked luminous. She was wearing a low-cut white cotton blouse over a short blue linen skirt and high heels. A modern goddess, thought Hamish. And then he saw the way Blair was staring at her and experienced a shiver of fear. No policeman of any intelligence can serve any time in the Highlands of Scotland without knowing a good deal about drunks. Drunks, thought Hamish bitterly, did not fall in love, they fell into obsession.

The look on Blair's face was a mixture of adoration, longing, and hunger. That was until his eyes turned on Charlie and burned with savage jealousy and hate.

He found Elspeth at his elbow. "Bad vibes, Hamish," she whispered. "I think it's the cat."

"Havers," said Hamish. "It's Blair. He wanted to kill Charlie before. Now he'll really try. But the pair are off to Uist the morn's morn." Elspeth was wondering whether to offer to stay the night when Priscilla walked in and Elspeth wondered how on earth Hamish could still light up at the very sight of her. Priscilla's present was a fine ram which she said was waiting at the hotel for Charlie. The colonel had said he would drive it to Uist in the horse trailer.

Oh, well, thought Elspeth. I'd be better off back in Glasgow anyway. But something made her say to Priscilla, "Have you taken a good look at that wild cat?"

"I popped into the vet's. Looks like Sonsie. Why?"

"I think there's something not right about it. I think it's someone who's come back."

"You don't believe that stuff, do you?" asked Priscilla. "I know some of the villagers think that the seals were people at one time."

Elspeth shrugged. "Just a bad feeling."

* * *

Hamish would have liked to stick closely to Charlie and Annie until he saw them off on the road to Uist the next day, but he knew he had better see Alison at eight in the evening and hope it wasn't another fantasy.

He dropped in to see the wild cat but it was still unconscious. He could not keep paying to keep it alive forever. Sooner or later, he must make up his mind to let it die.

As he walked along the waterfront, it was such a beautiful evening that he was reluctant to spoil it. The sea loch was like violet glass edged with pink in the setting sun. Little feathery clouds stretched across the sky. The forestry trees deepened to dark green and the heather on the flanks of the mountains became a softer purple. The villagers didn't have dinner in the evening: they had high tea consisting of one dish, scones, and cakes. The air still smelled of sugar and strong tea. Television sets flickered in parlours.

He approached Mrs. Mackenzie's boardinghouse, angry at Alison because he was sure she had nothing really interesting to tell him.

He rang the doorbell and waited. There was no reply. He was surprised because he knew Mrs. Mackenzie was nearly always home at this time of the evening. Callers were placed in a grim living room on the ground floor to wait. He tried the handle and found the door unlocked.

He walked in. The living room, or waiting room as he often thought of it, was empty. He could hear the faint sounds of a television set coming from a room off the hall: Mrs. Mackenzie's sanctum, as she liked to call it.

He recognised the back of Mrs. Mackenzie's head as she was sitting in a low-backed armchair. *Midsomer Murders* was showing.

"Mrs. Mackenzie!" called Hamish. No response. He went round and stood in front of her. Her eyes were closed and her breathing heavy. He felt her neck. There was a strong pulse. On a bamboo table beside her chair was a half-full glass of wine. He sniffed it cautiously. He tried to wake her without success. He phoned for an ambulance and then slowly mounted the stairs. A man in one of the rooms volunteered that Alison had the room at the end next to the fire escape. Hamish went along. No answer to his knock and her door was locked. He ran back to the kitchen where he knew the spare keys were up on a board and found the one to Alison's room. He ran back up and unlocked the door. Empty. Strong smell of cheap scent.

He went out and examined the fire escape and wished he had done so earlier because it was opened just a little, enough to let someone get back in. He would need to wait for the ambulance and put in a police report as well. He phoned Jimmy, who said the old girl was probably drunk but to let him know if it looked serious. The ambulance men arrived. Hamish bagged up the bottle for evidence and, having seen Mrs. Mackenzie borne off, went back up to the fire escape and studied the steps down. At the bottom there was still a damp patch of earth, and he saw the imprint of high heels in it. There was another patch by a gate in the hedge. Something had made Alison decide not to meet him.

A damp gust of wind blew against his cheek. He noticed choppy waves on the loch and black streamers of cloud like long grasping arms stretching in from the Atlantic.

* * *

Peter, the vet, thought he heard a movement from the surgery and went in before packing up for the night. But the cat lay still in its network of tubes.

* * *

Hamish decided to have one look at the peat bog before calling for a search party. Alison had wanted to tell him something and now she was missing. He began to run although his legs were still aching from the day's event. There lay the bog, the livid green moss surrounding it shining like emeralds in the encroaching gloom. And at the far edge, a weak movement. He took out his phone and called for the fire brigade and for backup. Then he lay on his stomach down beside the top of a head and sank his long arms down into the sludge of the bog. But he could not move her. The fire brigade had fortunately been called out on a false alarm in Lochdubh and so they arrived after only a few minutes, taking over just as the rain began to come down in sheets. This had the effect of loosening the body and they were able to drag it out. Alison's chalk-white face stared up at the tumbling clouds above, and rain washed the mud from her face. "She's got a wee bit o' a pulse," shouted a fireman. "Gie us the oxygen quick, Jimmy."

Hamish prayed all the way to the hospital.

CHAPTER SIX

And come he slow, or come he fast,
It is but Death who comes at last.

—Sir Walter Scott

By the time Hamish got back to the police station, he was shivering with cold, soaked to the skin. The initial report on Alison's condition was not good. Her nose and mouth had been blocked by the bog, and brain damage was feared. They had found her mobile phone in her pocket but it looked ruined and the forensic department sent it to a specialist in Glasgow in the hope of getting some information out of it. Mrs. Mackenzie was good news. She had woken in the hospital, furious. She had been taking sleeping pills because she had not been sleeping well.

He had a hot shower and scrubbed himself down with a rough towel. Then he made himself a cup of strong tea and settled himself on his battered sofa in his pyjamas and dressing gown, flicking through the channels in the hope of finding something on television that would take his mind off the murder. An advertisement crooned, "Why not leave your worries behind? Relax on one of our famous cruise ships..."

Hamish sat up straight. Why had Granny Dinwiddy, a self-centred old biddy if there ever was one, decided to throw herself overboard? And anyway, the steep fall from the ship would have killed her. She was blackmailing Paul English and Hamish was suddenly sure she was blackmailing other people as well. And what of this Mrs. Merriweather, the rich American? Had Granny Dinwiddy pushed her over and then taken her identity? The captain said they could sound alike, but that could have been part of the plot. If, say, Holly, the daughter, had murdered Paul, then he must have known something that had made them afraid.

Hamish felt he could not rest. He got dressed and drove over to police headquarters to demand the files on Granny Dinwiddy's suicide. The reports were thorough and painstaking. There was even an attached photo of the dead body and it could have been Granny Dinwiddy although the fish and the immersion in seawater had made a right mess of the body. There was a long statement from Mrs. Merriweather about how they had become close friends. Hamish leaned back, his hands clasped behind his head. So they had become close. That meant old Mrs. Dinwiddy would have been in and out of Mrs. Merriweather's cabin. Being a blackmailer, she probably automatically searched for incriminating letters. Or maybe she had thieved some jewellery and Mrs. Merriweather had caught her in the act. But there was certainly something fishy about the whole business. Mrs. Merriweather's third husband had died the year before, leaving her even richer than she had been made by the deaths of the previous two. Say she had staged the drowning to oblige Mrs. Dinwiddy. Could such an old lady survive the plunge from the deck? Not to mention the long swim to shore. Some corpse would have to be found but to a rich woman it would be easy enough to bribe someone at the morgue to find a homeless woman. He knew he was beginning to wander into the realms of fantasy but the Dinwiddys, mother and daughter, had proved to be blackmailers.

Of course he could get into trouble if he made an expensive phone call to the Houston police, but he was itching to get something, anything, to go on. In the morning he would get the daughter to explain where she was when Alison was attacked.

He expected to have to go in for long explanations but to his surprise he was put through to a Captain Dexter who said he had been suspicious of Mrs. Merriweather's late husbands' deaths. But the widow was protected by wealth and connections on all sides. He listened carefully to Hamish's suspicions and then said, "I'll get there now. You want to know if she's got a Scotch companion? And if she has, she could have helped her fake her suicide? Right. On it."

The evening drifted on. Hamish sat with his hands

clasped behind his head and wondered where Blair was and hoped Charlie was safe.

* * *

At that moment Priscilla was phoning her mother from London. "How's Pa?" she asked.

"He's on South Uist, darling, doing something with sheep."

"I hope you're not lonely."

"It's rather peaceful, you know. Poor George was always fretting. Now he doesn't."

"Is Hamish's cat still alive?"

"Last heard, it was. I took a look at the vet's the other day. Doesn't look like Sonsie to me."

"Nor me. I've a bad feeling about it."

"Oh, don't you start to go Highland on me. Your father will be believing in fairies soon. He's even taking lessons in Gaelic."

* * *

The phone on Hamish's desk rang shrilly, making him jump. It was the captain from Houston. "Well whaddya know?" he cried down the line.

"Tell me," urged Hamish.

"I call up with some talk about housebreakers and Mrs. Merriweather's there all right. I see a movement through in the kitchen so I say, 'I'll get a glass of water, ma'am.' She tried to stop me but she's overweight and in the kitchen here's this old woman and a younger one. I starts asking them if they're friends. Mrs. Merriweather's shouting to leave the staff alone. The one starts to talk with what she thinks is an American accent and ain't it Mrs. Dinwiddy. I'd dug up an old photo I got wired over on the supposed drowned woman and the old one is her to the life. I have a woman cop with me and we handcuff the pair and charge them while Merriweather is screaming that they forced her to do it. Took 'em all in."

Hamish begged him to e-mail a full report. Then after he had rung off, he realised the daughter couldn't have been murdering Alison if she was in Houston. He sighed and began to write out a full report. Jimmy came and sat beside him and goggled at the screen. "Good work, laddie," he exclaimed. "How did ye work all that out?"

"Because I never believed thon old biddy would take her own life. Who's guarding Alison at the hospital?"

"Blessed if I know. Blair took over."

"I'd better get over there. What was in the last report?"

"In a coma. But enough oxygen was cut off to damage her brain. They think if she does come out of the coma, she'll be a vegetable. Think she was blackmailing the murderer?"

"She's silly enough. Maybe she didn't know it was the murderer but someone she had seen that evening. Oh, well, I'm getting back to Lochdubh. I'm tired."

Jimmy watched him go. Then he erased Hamish's name from the report and put his own in instead.

He quickly switched off the computer as he saw Blair lumbering in and made his escape. Blair thought he could smell guilt. He switched on the computer, and the report now with Jimmy's name on it flashed up on the screen. Blair read it carefully. He dialled Houston police and got through to the captain who confirmed that a "smart cop," one Hamish Macbeth, had done a great bit of work.

Blair had been alarmed when it had looked as if Jimmy was in line to replace him, and so Blair phoned Daviot at home and—putting on a ponderous more-in-sorrow-than-in-anger voice—told his superior about Jimmy Anderson trying to gain undeserved credit. Having put the boot in for Jimmy tugged at Blair's reward syndrome. He *deserved* a drink. He rummaged through the desks until he found a quarter bottle of whisky and took one great slug of it, feeling his old friend coursing through his veins and demanding more. Out to the nearest pub and three doubles later, his mind was full of Annie. Soon would be the wedding and that must be stopped. Charlie must be made to have an accident. That shooting idea had been crazy: all the fault of those weird drugs. He'd stick to whisky from now on. He was wafted off on dreams of Annie. They would get married and he would lead a decent life, a life worthy of her. He never stopped for a moment to wonder what he was supposed to do about his wife, Mary. He decided to go to Uist the following day and see what damage he could do.

* * *

Hamish had a sudden feeling that he should go to Braikie and check on Alison but it was three in the morning and his muscles were aching from the running and he was exhausted.

* * *

A silent figure crept along the deserted nighttime corridors of Braikie hospital. No guard on Alison's room. The door quietly opened and a shadowy figure slipped in and reached for the tubes connected to Alison's body. But approaching footsteps sounded and the figure hid behind a screen and then decided to escape. Try again the next day.

* * *

Jimmy was already on the carpet for having tried to thieve Hamish's detective work. He was protesting that Blair had done it himself in order to discredit Hamish. Daviot tugged his grey hair and felt he should be a tougher man and appoint Hamish up the ranks. Creeps such as Blair kept weak men like himself in power, as he realised in his odd moment of self-introspection. Hamish Macbeth was a truly unambitious man, and such men were almost impossible to understand. What was the point of having flashes of brilliance and not using them to further one's career? And why had Blair chosen this day of all days to go missing?

* * *

Blair was on the ferry from Oban to South Uist, feeling like some mediaeval knight. Annie should be saved from a cloth-headed lump like Charlie Carter. He planned to lure Charlie out of the caravan after dark, forgetting it was still high summer and the nights never got dark.

Inside his little caravan, George got ready for bed. He considered himself a very lucky man and was well aware that most newly engaged women would not have tolerated his presence. But Annie was as friendly and laid-back as her husband. That his wife did not seem to mind his absence did not give him a moment's thought. He was well aware the marriage was arranged because of his money, and after the miracle of Priscilla's birth they had lived together more as brother and sister.

Blair had the plot clear in his head. He would set fire to the couple's van. Shoot Charlie when he emerged and he would say…he would say…

It was as if a great tide of madness suddenly rolled from his brain, leaving him sober and very afraid. He clearly saw the investigation that would follow. His car had been seen on the ferry. He had bought petrol at the local garage.

* * *

"Hamish's cat is dead," said the vet to his assistant. "Right glad I am, too. You would think there was something nasty emanating from it. I swear that isnae Sonsie, but Hamish won't listen to me."

Suddenly the cat twitched and opened a slit of yellow in one eye. "Oh, the damn thing's come back to the land of the living. I should pull out the tubes and save Hamish some money, but I havenae killed an animal yet and I don't mean to start."

* * *

Hamish went to Braikie hospital the following day, phoned headquarters for a guard on Alison, and was told to guard her himself, as they were short of men. He settled in a chair outside and wondered if they planned to send relief.

A sympathetic nurse brought him coffee and a newspaper. It was sunny outside and the air in the corridor was soporific. His eyelids began to droop. Soon he was fast asleep.

He was awoken five minutes later by a voice demanding, "How is the patient?"

A policeman was standing in front of him, questioning an Asian doctor. "So far, so good," said the doctor. "I mean, she's still alive, but whether her brain will ever function again properly is another question."

He walked off and Hamish and the policeman surveyed each other. "I'm your new assistant," said the policeman. "Larry Coomb."

Hamish reflected that Larry looked about fourteen years old with his rosy cheeks and mop of curly brown hair. "Are you moving into the police station?" asked Hamish. "Because I'll need to finish clearing out the spare bedroom for you."

"I'll live in that B and B along by the bridge where Alison lived until you're ready for me."

"Grand," said Hamish. "Off you go. Come back and do a late shift for me, say midnight to six, and then I'll take over again."

Hamish felt the day drag on and wished he had asked Larry to come back earlier. The library trolley came round and so he selected *War and Peace,* that book that sooner or later most of the reading population vows they will finish. He was just considering why the Russians didn't make it easier by sticking to one name when Larry came back, carrying a container of coffee and a Danish. "I'm all set," Larry remarked. "I'll phone if there's anything." His voice was lowland Scots.

"Where are you from?" asked Hamish.

"Montrose."

"Pretty down there."

"Aye, but I got lassie trouble. She says I was going to marry her and I said nothing of the kind so I opted to get as far away as possible."

"Don't mess with the locals," said Hamish. "It's a small world up here. I'll be back at six in the morning."

When Hamish had gone, Larry ate his Danish and

started to read the copy of *War and Peace* that Hamish had left behind. By two in the morning, he was fast asleep.

Something woke him an hour later. He sensed a movement to his right. But before he could leap to his feet, a bedpan was brought down crashing onto his skull, crushing it, and he slumped to the ground.

Two minutes later the lifeless body of Alison lay in a welter of pulled-out tubes and a figure slipped quietly away into the night.

* * *

Hamish was roused before dawn by a hysterical call from the hospital and alerted headquarters before driving to Braikie. The news was as bad as could be. Not only was Alison dead but it was touch and go with Larry Coomb and doubtful if he would be any more than a vegetable if he survived.

A forensic team were busy and he retreated with Jimmy to the canteen. "Nobody saw anything," said Jimmy gloomily. "CCTV? Forget it. Doesnae work. Och, what's going on here? The whole thing is weird. I phoned Blair and he says in this scary-polite voice, 'I will be over later, Anderson, but I trust you to handle it in your usual competent manner.'"

"I'm right glad to hear he's in Strathbane and not over in Uist trying to kill Charlie," said Hamish. "There seems to be madness all around. This killer is an amateur who just takes chances. And is getting away with it. We've been thinking that English was killed because of his rudeness but it could be something in his past. I'll need all the reports from Stirling. Maybe there's someone he made bankrupt. Something like that."

"You should be down questioning the staff," said Jimmy.

"You've got a whole team doing that," Hamish pointed out. "Let me go back to the station and read all the notes about when he was a bank manager. It's just a hunch."

"Oh, all right. But if Blair comes chapping at the door, pretend you're out."

* * *

It was a grey misty day as if in mourning for the young policeman who, it appeared, might not survive. As Hamish approached Lochdubh, he was aware of an odd feeling of menace in the air and gave a superstitious shiver.

He entered the police station cautiously but there was only Lugs to bark a welcome. Hamish made a pot of strong coffee, fed Lugs some sausages, and settled down at the computer in his office. After an hour of searching, he found one possibility. A local Stirling shopkeeper had been made bankrupt and had hanged himself. He had left a suicide note in which he blamed Paul English. Hamish reached for the phone to call Stirling police but then hesitated. He longed to interview the family himself. He read more of the notes and his eyes brightened. Why had that not been noticed before? His wife and son had moved to Crask up the coast, only a short drive away.

He put Lugs in the front seat of the Land Rover and phoned Jimmy. "Did no one follow up the Crask lead?" he asked. "Who was on it?"

"MacNab. But he was about to go when Blair was accused and then I think it got forgotten. Let me know if you get anything."

Hamish drove on. He parked in the little main street of Crask. The mist had got thicker and seemed to blot out all sound. He went into the general store and asked directions to Lorne Road and was told it was two streets to the right as you left the shop.

The house was on a council estate. Often people who lived on estates such as these bought their homes and the whole place took on a prosperous look, but this one had an air of decay and hopelessness about it. The gardens did not boast flowers or plants but pieces of rusting machinery or old cars. He squinted at his piece of paper. Mrs. Trimble. He hoped she was at home.

At first it seemed as if she had gone out. He knocked again, loudly, and shouted, "Police!"

A light went on upstairs. Then the curtains were drawn back, the window opened, and a frowsty, bloated-looking woman stared down. "Gie me a moment," she shouted.

It was more like twenty minutes before the front door opened and she ushered him into a front room. Hamish waited patiently while she darted about, picking up magazines and empty cider bottles and stacking them in a corner.

"Sit doon," she ordered in a rasping voice. She had a sagging figure in harem pants and a T-shirt. Her blonde hair showed black at the roots, and her face was crisscrossed with red broken veins. "So what's our Bertha been up to?"

"Bertha?"

"My daughter. She's in Glasgow. Got done for drugs last week."

"It's not about her," said Hamish. "It is about Paul English."

"Paul…Oh, yon sod. Made us broke. We had a wee toy shop. Was all right but we let folk run up a bill at Christmas and pay in the next few months. We asked thon bank manager as usual to wait and he ups and makes us bankrupt. My man took tae the bottle and then topped hisself. I went down tae that bank and told English I'd kill him. He called the polis on me. Bastard! You find out who killed him and I'll shake that man by the hand, so I will."

"Have you ever visited Lochdubh?" asked Hamish.

"Aye, I went down tae yon peat bog where he was found dead. I wanted to check out he really was dead."

"But were you in, say, Cnothan, before he died? Or did you meet him?"

"Hadnae a clue where he'd gone until I heard about the murder. We were a good family and he wrecked us. Bertha on the streets and me rotting away in this dump."

"Can you think of anyone else from the Stirling days that might actually have murdered him?"

"I could think better, sonny, wi' a wee drap o' cider in me."

"Wait."

Hamish went back to the shop and bought a bottle of cider, feeling guilty, but trying to persuade himself it was for the better good.

"Ta." She seized the bottle, unscrewed the top and took a massive slug, slowly wiped her mouth with the back of one fat, swollen red hand, and said, "I call tae mind he had this fiancée. Whit was the lassie's name? La de da. Schoolteacher. He dumped her, she took an overdose but got pumped out. Left Stirling. Caro something or other."

* * *

Hamish drove back to Lochdubh and to his notes. He phoned the school and found out that a Miss Caro Fleming had left several years ago and last heard was resident in Helmsdale but they did not have her address.

As he took the long drive to the east coast and Lochdubh fell behind him, the mist began to thin and disappear and he had an odd feeling of having escaped from some sort of evil.

Lugs began to wag his plume of a tail and Hamish realised for the first time that his dog had been very subdued the last few months and maybe had been missing Sonsie more than he had thought.

He was wearing civilian clothes because he did not want to offend any local copper by appearing to poach on his beat. But no one seemed to have heard of a Caro Fleming, the sun had come out, and the day was sticky and warm. Hamish stopped in a café and ordered a pot of tea. As a faint hope, he asked the woman serving him if she knew of a Caro Fleming. She looked surprised and said, "That's me."

Hamish produced his warrant card and asked her if he could have a chat about Paul English. Two women came in and Caro said, "Not now. I close up at six o' clock. Come back then."

Hamish was relieved that Caro showed no signs of having taken to drink or drugs. She was a tall, flat-chested woman with a long face like that in a Modigliani painting and she had long thin hands and feet.

He looked at his watch. Only half an hour to wait and the tea was very good. With Lugs at his feet, Hamish felt at ease for the first time in months.

* * *

"I hope this won't be too painful for you," he began, "but I am investigating the murder of Paul English and I would like to know a bit more about his character."

"He was a rude, cruel, and unfeeling bastard. All that man ever loved was money. It's only amazing that he hadn't robbed his own bank. I tell you, he wore an anorak with an inside pocket and in that pocket he kept a wad of banknotes. Said he liked to feel them next to his heart. And to think I nearly married him!"

"What stopped you?"

"Wait till I close up. It's a quiet day anyway." She put the CLOSED sign on the door and came back and sat down. "More tea?"

"Yes, please."

"So, it was the week afore the wedding. I was paying. 'Lash out,' says he. 'Wear white. I want the world to know I've bagged the prize.' Now Maggie Friend, her what runs the chippy along the road, she's aye been jealous of me. 'It's your money he wants,' says she. 'Betcha he's got you to make out a will in his favour already.' Well, you know something? He had. But he was so loving, I couldn't believe it. It was when he found out I was going to wear a second-hand dress and said I should wear only the best and I could afford it, I said I had always been canny with money and I'd seen this programme about starving children and so I had changed my will to leave all my money to the charity." A tear ran down her long nose and plopped onto the tablecloth. "That's when he told me straight that his only interest in me was money. He dragged me over to the mirror and jeered at my reflection. Then he walked out and that was the last I saw of him. I'm glad he's dead."

Hamish patiently asked her where she had been on the night Paul was murdered and she said she had been at a choir rehearsal in the church. "I had a lucky escape," she said sadly, "even though it was so humiliating. He was a dirty beast."

* * *

Hamish drove slowly back to Lochdubh. He realised he had always imagined the murderer would turn out to be a man.

But what if it was a woman? What of the minister that the little girl claimed to have seen with Paul in the vestry? He was sure if he tried to talk to her again, all that it would gain for the lassie was another beating. He turned off, took the road to Cnothan, and stopped outside the manse.

The minister, Maisie Walters, answered the door. "Oh, it's you," she said. "Jake and I were about to have supper. Can you come back tomorrow?"

"It is just the one question," said Hamish. "May I come in?" Jake, he wondered. Who is Jake?

"For a moment." She stood aside. Hamish removed his cap and walked into the front room where a table was set at the bay window. A small grey-haired man rose at his entrance.

"This is one of our elders, Jake Ingles," said Maisie. "What do you want to know?"

"I don't think you have ever been asked. Where were you the night Paul English was murdered?"

"Good heavens!" cried Jake. "Never say you suspect our minster!"

"Mrs. Walters?"

"I was working in my study on a sermon. Before that I'd taken evening service. My car was parked outside here where anyone could see it. The light was on in the study and anyone passing would have seen me at the desk by the window. Now, if that is all, our supper is getting cold. Do not come back without a good reason."

"One more thing. Where were you last night? Did you go to Braikie?"

"I was here in my bed."

Hamish walked to the doorway and then turned around. "Did Paul English ever ask you to make out a will in his favour?"

"Why would he do that?"

"Seemed to make a habit of it," said Hamish, studying her face.

"Nonsense. Now if you've quite finished..."

Hamish left. He was sure she had been lying.

* * *

As he drove down into Lochdubh, he could feel menace in the very air. He stopped on the waterfront where Archie Maclean was sitting on the wall, smoking a cigarette. Hamish had a sudden sharp longing for a cigarette but fought against it. He lifted Lugs out and then joined Archie on the seawall.

"Grand evening," said Hamish.

"Aye. Good few tourists this year, but something's bad."

"Like what?"

"Folk are sniping and bitching."

"Why?"

"Dinnae ask me. It's something in the air."

"Unsolved murders poison the very atmosphere," said Hamish.

"How's yon cat?"

"Hanging in there. I'll need to make a decision soon. What do you know of the minister at Cnothan?"

"Mrs. Walters? Not much. You should be asking our minister."

"Should ha' thought o' that. I'll go now."

* * *

Mrs. Wellington, the minister's wife, answered the door and glared up at Hamish. "If you've come mooching for a free coffee, you are not getting one."

"I've come to see the minister," said Hamish. "For heffen's sake, woman, now I've seen everything. You're wearing a tweed pinafore."

"It is just an old bit of cloth," said Mrs Wellington, who was famous for always being clad in tweed, winter or summer. "You'll find Mr. Wellington in the study."

Mr. Wellington looked up from writing a sermon as Hamish entered. "Thinking about getting married again?" he asked. "Just my little joke. I can see it's not that."

Hamish removed his cap and ran a hand through his fiery hair. "What do you know about the minister Mrs. Walters?"

"Not very much. I was surprised because I took services at Cnothan as well as here. But she seemed determined to get the church. I believe she preaches very impassioned sermons. She does not like sex."

"In what way?"

"I gather she thinks it should be confined to the marriage bed. She is constantly writing letters to the newspapers and television complaining about nudity and explicit sex."

"Odd coming from a woman who's been married."

"Well, do you know, but it is a sad thing, there are still women who are so horrified by their introduction to intercourse that they say 'Never again.'" The minister looked sad. Bet that's what happened to you, thought Hamish. Then he thought of Priscilla's coldness and wondered again if something had happened to her long before he knew her to make her so passionless.

"Would you say such as Maisie Walters could murder someone?"

"Frankly, no. She is too self-satisfied and always right. I think he was murdered by someone in a rage."

"Unfortunately, he put so many people in a rage, I don't know where to start. And while the murderer is out there, there's this nasty feeling all round the village."

"It's the violet nights," said Mr. Wellington, half to himself. "It never gets really dark in summer, just this odd gloaming. People think that's when the fairies come out. I'll try to think of something for the community to do. Some charity work to bring us all together."

"Let me know when you do," said Hamish.

* * *

Charlie and Annie were married in Lochdubh church on a fine summer's day. Annie wore a white wedding dress of silk chiffon and had a coronet of pearls lent to her by Mrs. Halburton-Smythe on her head. They came from miles around. The celebrations went all night and into the next day. Priscilla tried to suggest to her father that he might leave the couple alone for a few weeks but he said they didn't mind and so eventually went off in the wedding limousine, sitting in the back with the poodle on his knee.

Hamish wondered who headquarters would send to replace Charlie. The spare bedroom at the station was now full of junk and he would have to clear it out. He realised with a pang that he was going to miss Charlie's good-natured company. The news about Larry Coomb's possible recovery was more hopeful.

* * *

A week after the wedding, he was strolling along the water-front when his eye was caught by a poster wrapped round a lamppost. It said, HELP RAISE FUNDS TO SAVE THE CAT.

"Mr. Wellington's idea," said Angela Brodie as she walked up to him. "We all know it's costing a lot. There's to be a ceilidh in the church hall this Saturday. Mr. Patel is cooking up haggis burgers. Mrs. Halburton-Smythe has contributed three cases of prosciutto because she says it's cheap rubbish and they shouldn't be serving it at the castle. It's ten pounds a ticket. There's even two coachloads from Inverness coming up for the shindig."

"If it gets out that Sonsie is a wild cat, I'll be in trouble," said Hamish.

"Don't worry. No one's going to blab."

"Oh, dear," said Hamish. "Now I feel guilty. If it was for starving kids in Africa, there wouldn't be this interest. It's always animals that people are prepared to pay to rescue."

"Cheer up. It's being done for the village more than you. There's been a bad atmosphere in Lochdubh."

* * *

Mrs. Wellington had thawed and given the money-raising venture her blessing when she realised she and her line dancers could put on their Stetsons and fringed skirts and perform to "All My Exes Live in Texas."

The Currie sisters were to be allowed to sing one verse of "Come into the Garden, Maud," and the local schoolchildren were to perform the Scottish dance the Petronella. Then the buffet would be declared open and after that, dancing for all.

To Hamish's delight, Charlie and Annie phoned to say they would be there, and Dick and Anka from the bakery were also coming and contributing trays of cakes.

The party was well under way when the door of the church hall opened and Detective Chief Inspector Blair walked in. Behind him came Jimmy Anderson, who went quickly to Hamish's side. "Dinnae fash yerself, laddie," he whispered. "He's like a lamb these days."

And sure enough, Blair didn't drink anything stronger than Coke and after fifteen minutes took his leave. He had not looked at Annie once.

"Isn't your pal George coming?" Hamish asked Charlie.

"There's a wee bit o' trouble there," said Charlie. "There's this widow, Fran Mackay, near us in Uist and she's set her cap at George."

"Does she know he's married?"

"'Course she does. Annie told her straight. But she's got these great boobs and they seem to fascinate George. He's beginning to think his wife wouldn't mind a divorce."

"Can't he have an affair?"

"George is hardly the affair type o' fellow."

"Is he still a snob?"

"Not when it comes to me!"

"Aye, but he always liked the lords and ladies."

"I suppose he always will. Hated being associated with trade."

"What about if the Earl of Strawban issued an invitation? That would get him out on the road for a bit."

"Could you wangle that?"

"I've still got that silver cup I won at his clay pigeon shoot. The winner is supposed to keep it but he wants it back. I'll tell him he can have it if he invites George."

* * *

It was as if the fund-raising to save Sonsie had lifted the bad feeling from the village. Hamish was delighted to hear that it looked as if Larry would make a complete recovery although it would take some time.

CHAPTER SEVEN

The best laid schemes o' mice and men,
Gang aft a-gley.

—Robert Burns

The nights were beginning to draw in and the mountains blazed purple with heather. Hamish heard that Priscilla was at Tommel Castle and made his way there. He found her helping in the gift shop. "Up for long?" he asked. She looked as perfect as ever with the smooth bell of her blonde hair and her slim figure in a cashmere blue jersey and skirt.

"Just the weekend. Mother's a bit upset."

"What's up?"

"Well, she thought Pa was over in Uist haunting Charlie and drove over but Charlie said he'd gone back to the mainland and Mother said that Charlie and Annie looked decidedly shifty. She's looking through the stuff on his desk to see if he left a clue as to where he was going. You look stricken. Know anything about this?"

"Me? No. I'll just be having a word with Mr. Johnson."

* * *

Hamish found the manager in his office. "Do you know where the boss has gone?" he asked.

"No, but he was stinking of Tiger Balm aftershave—you know, that stuff teenage boys put on because they think it attracts the lassies."

Hamish had a sinking feeling. He was suddenly sure that George had taken the widow and her boobs to the earl's home.

"When did he leave?"

"Yesterday."

He was just leaving the hotel when Mrs. Halburton-Smythe hailed him. She held out a letter. "Do you know anything about this? It's an invitation to Strawban's place but George never said a word."

"He maybe thought you were still away."

"Don't be silly. He's the one that's always away, playing a sort of Robinson Crusoe over in Uist. I'll phone Emily and ask her what the hell is going on."

Hamish headed for the door. "Wait a moment, Hamish," she called. "I may need your help."

She rang and Hamish heard her side of the conversation. "George is there with his secretary? Indeed? This must be a new venture. Yes, I'll be there around early evening. Oh, she does, does she. Well, I'll bring Macbeth as well."

When she rang off, Mrs. Halburton-Smythe fixed Hamish with a gimlet stare. "George is parading some female as his secretary and she says she is your cousin."

"Not guilty," said Hamish.

"Really? Well, you're coming with me to sort this out. Who is she?"

"She's a widow called Fran Mackay who has set her cap at your husband. He's probably flattered. I'll get rid of her for you."

* * *

It was worse than Hamish could have thought. Instead of being spurned as a common interloper, Fran Mackay appeared to have charmed the Strawbans.

She had a great head of straw-coloured hair, rosy cheeks, and two magnificent white breasts partly exposed by a low-necklined blouse. Her voice had the musical lilt of the isles. She had just been showing Lady Strawban an intricate knitting stitch, and Lady Strawban—who was an avid knitter—was hanging on her every word. The earl was gazing at those bosoms with a silly smile on his face. Only George looked stricken and miserable at the sight of his wife.

Hamish and Mrs. Halburton-Smythe stayed for tea and then she surprised Hamish by saying casually that she would see her husband sometime or another.

As they walked out to her car, Mrs. Halburton-Smythe said, "George really doesn't have much fun. He won't actually do anything. I mean, he's never been unfaithful to me. You young people, it's all romance with you. But for us it was a business arrangement. People think that girls marrying for money belongs to the dark ages, but in my day you owed it to your parents."

"What's really the trouble with Priscilla?" asked Hamish abruptly.

"You will need to ask her."

"I've tried."

"Then leave my daughter alone and find someone else. Everyone expects you to marry Elspeth Grant. Why don't you?"

"She won't move back here and I don't want to go to Glasgow."

"How's your cat?"

"Still the same."

"Some of the villagers are saying it isn't Sonsie."

"Rubbish. I know my own cat."

"The older people think it is lying there, emanating evil."

Hamish shrugged. "Half o' them still believe in fairies."

* * *

The colonel returned to the hotel that evening, looking sheepish. It turned out that Fran had been asked to stay on with the Strawbans. George seemed surprised at this. Being English he could never quite accustom himself to the democratic views of the Scottish aristocracy.

On impulse Hamish asked him to visit the police station and look at some murder case notes. George was thrilled. He longed to play Poirot. He sat in the office carefully scrutinising Hamish's notes and at the end of several hours said, "Well, it is all very simple."

Hamish looked amused. "Well, O Great Detective. Tell me who done it so we can get to bed."

"It's the forestry workers," said George. "They attacked him. They went back and chucked him in the bog when you weren't there. Simple."

"I'd like to think so," said Hamish cautiously. "But I am sure he phoned someone. It may have been someone he had been having an affair with that he didn't want anyone else to know about, and he had a throwaway phone."

"I think you're wrong," said George stubbornly. "I am sure Charlie would agree with me."

Hamish suddenly wished Charlie had not left to get married. He missed his easy-going company. George said he was going to Uist the following day because he had supplies to take to Charlie. "I wish I could go with you," said Hamish, "but I've a mind to go round the hospital again. I wonder if the police looked at any CCTV cameras from the streets near the hospital."

* * *

When Hamish entered police headquarters the first person he saw was Blair. To his amazement, Blair merely nodded to him and walked away. The detective had also slimmed down considerably and his face was free of the marks of heavy drinking. In any other man, Hamish would believe some rehab had worked its magic, but in Blair's case it was almost as if, without him knowing it, he was sobering up for something. All Hamish could hope was that the something wasn't an attack on Charlie.

A policewoman dug out CCTV tapes that had been collected and placed them on a desk for him to view. Solve the murder of Alison, thought Hamish. And then I'll know who killed Paul English.

The tapes were old and grainy and showed all the signs of having been reused over and over again. But at least when Alison was murdered, the summer nights were still light with that odd violet gloaming. Would the murderer have calmly walked in the front entrance? Very few people came and went, mostly staff standing outside smoking, despite a large notice which warned that no smoking was permitted on the hospital grounds. There were no cameras at the sides or back of the hospital. Hamish put in a tape for Glebe Street, the broad street that ran along the outside of the hospital. An ambulance raced up; a body was lifted out, the face covered by an oxygen mask. Hamish stifled a yawn as he continued to watch. Then he suddenly wound back the tape. A shadowy figure slid out of the hospital and disappeared up the side into the tree-covered shadows. Could be either a man or a woman, he thought. He froze the picture and leaned back in his chair, his hands clasped behind his head. "If I wanted to get right into the hospital," he said aloud, "I might fake a heart attack. When they had put me in some bed to wait for a doctor, I'd simply get up and find where Alison was, which they made easy on the final attempt, with the policeman outside. So that's how it might have been done," he concluded. "Fake a heart attack and get an ambulance to take you in."

He was unaware that Blair had been standing behind him. The detective went upstairs and into Daviot's office. He told him that he had been studying the CCTV footage and he thought that the murderer might have faked a heart attack to get carried in. After the first attempt on Alison, everyone would have been alerted.

"Good work, Blair," said Daviot. "Keep at it!"

* * *

Blair went back downstairs and told Hamish that Daviot had heard he was in headquarters and had ordered that he return to his beat. "Sorry about that, old son," said Blair. "Leave the videos and I'll get someone to put them away."

"I think I should tell the boss that I need more time. I mean, Braikie is on my beat."

Something unlovely suddenly peered out of Blair's eyes. "Do as you are ordered, sonny," he said.

* * *

Hamish raced for Braikie with the siren blaring. He wanted to get there before Blair because Blair would be keen to follow up that lead. He found out the name of the ambulance driver who had brought in the heart attack. He was in their office, having a break.

To Hamish's questions, he said, "Aye, it was a wee man. We gave him oxygen and rushed him off."

"Name and address?" asked Hamish eagerly.

"Got it in the book. Here we are. John Clarke, number five, Orchard Road. Nurse says she went to move him to a bed and he had disappeared."

"Was he in the house or out in the garden when you called?" asked Hamish.

"He was hanging ower the garden gate."

Hamish felt excited. This so-called John Clarke possibly had found an empty house and pretended it was his own by waiting in the garden and then faking a heart attack.

He said, "Be careful. There's a man pretending to be a detective chief inspector called Blair. Don't tell him anything."

* * *

Hamish raced to Orchard Road. The house was a villa with a large front garden full of thick bushes and trees. He went up to the front door and rang the bell. The door was answered by a small man with grey hair. "Mr. Clarke?"

"The same. What's up?"

"Did you call an ambulance recently?"

"Aye, I was in the garden, weeding, and I came over faint. But they left me lying in a hard bed and I thought, och, I'm okay. So I just walked home."

Dead end, thought Hamish gloomily. But he said, "You'll have heard about the murder and the attack on that poor policeman. Did you see anyone suspicious?"

"No, not a soul. As I walked out, I could hear a lot of screaming."

"Look, a man pretending to be a detective will call soon. Don't tell him anything."

"Look, mac, I won't even answer the door."

* * *

Shortly after Hamish had left, Blair arrived. He could see Clarke inside but the man made no attempt to answer the door. Guilty as hell, thought Blair. He called for backup and when it arrived told the man with the battering ram to break in.

That was when Mr. Clarke had a genuine heart attack through sheer fright and had to be taken off in an ambulance. The ambulance men asked the detective if his name was Blair and, getting the affirmative, threw Blair to the ground and handcuffed him with his own handcuffs. It took some time from members of the backup team to convince them that Blair was the genuine article.

Blair was about to put in a report that all this misery had been caused by Hamish Macbeth—but if he did that,

Hamish would reveal that it was his idea that Clarke might be the murderer.

He longed to go to the pub but knew he would not leave until he was well and truly drunk, and he thirsted for revenge on Hamish. He was no longer obsessed with Annie since he had thrown away those madness-inducing pills. But Hamish was another matter. He nursed all the humiliations he had experienced at Hamish's hands. All he needed to do was manufacture a simple accident. He wistfully remembered the days before the booze had taken over his life. He had been a good detective.

He suddenly had a mad brain wave. He would go over every note on the murders and find out the name of the killer, and then he would do a deal: *I will not arrest you if you kill Hamish Macbeth. Just don't murder anyone else.* Foolproof!

Mary Blair became uneasy about her husband. Not only was he sober but he was bringing work home. She was used to expertly handling a drunk, but this sober Blair who barked orders at her she found scary.

One morning she headed over to the police station in Lochdubh and found Hamish drinking coffee in the kitchen, reading the local paper. "Pull up a chair and have some coffee," said Hamish. "What brings you? Is he drunk again?"

"I wish he were," said Mary. "He's scary-sober and works in the evenings going over all the notes about the murders."

Hamish's hazel eyes sharpened. "Does he now. Ambition rears its ugly head at last. You know, he hasnae tried to get back to South Uist. Any sign he's still obsessed wi' Annie?"

"No, he said a lassie in love with a moron like Charlie isnae worth bothering about."

"Sour grapes?"

"Oh, no, he meant it. I said I was taking a run over to Lochdubh because Patel has some special deals, and he said I was to get into the police station. If you had any notes on the murders, I was to swipe them and bring them back with me."

"What's he about? He knows I never take the credit. He wishes I were dead. He..."

Hamish's mouth fell open and he stared blankly at Mary.

She waved a hand in front of his face. "Planet Earth to Hamish Macbeth. Come in please."

Hamish blinked and then said, "Mention me much, does he?"

"Mutters under his breath. 'That'll fix that red-haired bastard. I wonder if I could be there.' Things like that."

"Now, the only place your man would want to be with me there would be if I were dying. Try this, Mary. He finds out the murderer and does a deal: *You off Hamish Macbeth and I won't charge you.*"

"That's mad."

"Aye but this is your husband we're talking about. His brain hasnae recovered from those damn pills."

"Oh, I could cope when he was just your old-fashioned drunk," moaned Mary. "I knew how to handle him."

"Couldn't you have a word with Mrs. Daviot?"

"Then I think I'd be the one that'd end up dead."

"I'll give you a copy of some of the notes," said Hamish. "You'd better start giving me a daily report. Your man used to be a good detective, and I could do wi' all the help I can get."

* * *

After Mary had left, Hamish reflected on the odd situation and thought that Blair was rather like a rabid dog. But he was relieved that Blair's obsession with Annie had fizzled out. Who would headquarters send to replace him? Then he thought, Blair will try to get some creature to do his bidding, someone who will report if I have any progress in solving the murders. In any case, it'll be some awful creep.

* * *

Because Larry would not be returning, the policeman Blair was determined would replace Charlie was a small man called Silas Dunbar. He looked too small to be a policeman but he had just scraped past the regulation height; it was his cringing air that made him seem smaller. He had sandy hair and pale-green eyes which peered out at the world with a furtive look. His nose was sharp and curved and his mouth small and tucked in at the corners. He lived with his mother in a flat in Strathbane. He could not remember his father, who died when Silas was two years old.

His mother was large and bosomy and domineering. It

was she who decided that Silas must become a policeman. To make sure she knew what he was up to at all times, she waylaid Blair one day and explained who she was and what her concerns were. Blair immediately saw the possibility of having someone spy on Macbeth and persuaded her that Silas's road to promotion could be through Lochdubh. Normally Mrs. Edith Dunbar would not have relished the idea of her son having any freedom at all, but she had lately joined a country dancing class and had her eyes on a widower and a sudden yen to get married again.

And so one sunny morning Silas drove his old Ford over the hills and moors and cruised down into Lochdubh. Reluctant to spoil the day by reporting immediately to the police station, Silas parked on the waterfront and got out and looked around. Little white clouds like feathers covered the sky and were reflected in the mirror surface of the sea loch. The small whitewashed cottages with their flower-filled gardens formed a curve, and at the harbour tourists were getting ready to board Archie's fishing boat. He wished he had never joined the police force and had become a crofter or a forestry worker and lived free of shackles in a place like this. He had his firm instructions to spy on Macbeth and put in a report at the end of each week.

He reluctantly got back into his car and drove to the police station, parking it outside behind the Land Rover.

He opened the garden gate and knocked on the door under the blue lamp, almost hidden under a cascade of red rambling roses.

"Kitchen door at the side," a voice shouted.

Silas made his way around the side of the building to the kitchen door, which was standing open. Hamish was in civilian clothes. "So you're Dunbar," he said. "We'll deal with your bags later. I'm hungry and it's lunchtime so I'll treat you to a meal at the Italian's. Come on, Lugs."

Bemused, Silas followed the tall red-haired sergeant and his odd-looking blue-eyed dog. "The murders are, of course, top priority," Hamish said. "But we still have a lot of irritating wee cases and the whole o' Sutherland to patrol."

They found a table at the window. Willie Lamont, who had once been Hamish's policeman, fussed around them, cleaning the table and even the menus until Hamish sharply told him to take their order. Willie had married the restaurant owner's daughter and entered into a blissful life of discovering new cleaners. While they were waiting for their food, Hamish studied Silas. His shoulders were hunched and his eyes were on the table.

"Why on earth did you join the police force?" asked Hamish. "Willie! Bring us a bottle o' Valpolicella."

"Yis shouldnae drink on duty."

"We're not on duty. Hop to it."

"I don't drink alcohol," said Silas.

"Alcoholic?"

"No."

"So why?"

Silas hung his head. "My mother signed me up for the Temperance Society."

"Did she now? Well, she isn't here and a glass won't kill ye."

The bay window of the restaurant was open, and smells of pine, salt, tar, and afternoon baking drifted lazily in.

They had both ordered one main dish of veal Marsala. Silas took a gulp of wine and screwed up his face. It tasted sour. But a warmth spread up from his stomach and he had a sudden desire to cry. He was wrestling with his conscience because he did not want to spy on this kind sergeant.

Hamish studied his face for a few moments and then said, "He's done it before, you know. We are talking here about Detective Chief Inspector Blair, who has no doubt ordered you to spy on me?"

"Yes, but I can resign from the force," said Silas.

"No, no, calm down. Take it easy. I'll do the reports for you. Settle in. Have more wine. Eat your food. Those are my orders. Maybe there's something in those interviews done by detectives and other coppers. I mean, after Paul's body had been found, the place was flooded with police asking questions. I've been concentrating too much on my own notes."

"I went to Mrs. Mackenzie's before I heard there was room for me in the station," said Silas. "I'm glad I'm not staying there. All those religious texts on the walls. At least she's the sort of God-fearing woman who wouldn't dream of withholding evidence."

"I wonder," said Hamish. "What would make her hold her tongue? Threats? No. She'd play the martyr. Let's have some pudding and then go back and find out what she did say."

Silas had drunk nearly half a bottle of wine and longed to go to bed but felt better after Hamish had made him a strong cup of coffee. They sat at the desk in the office and Hamish scanned through the various reports until he said at last, "Here we are. Interviewed by Jimmy Anderson, no less."

"Did they find his mobile?" asked Silas.

"No, the rain came back and nearly killed Blair, who was jumping up and down. Let's see. Mrs. Mackenzie outraged that anyone should even suggest there were shenanigans going on in her respectable establishment. Oh, I did read this but it was her usual moan. I should have known from another case that she takes sleeping pills. What about the forestry workers who stay there? I mean it was forestry workers who assaulted English in the first place. Yes, it seems they all knew Alison had a habit of nipping out through the fire escape. But not one of them ever saw her meeting a man. Back to Jimmy. Now, here's a thing. Jimmy says that the last time he was in Mrs. Mackenzie's parlour she still had an ancient TV set. He says this time she had the latest flat-screen. So let's fantasise. Someone knows something and Mrs. Mackenzie might tell the police and so that would explain the bribe of a good television set."

"If Jimmy noticed the television then he must have thought it was suspicious."

"Not if a football match was on. So we'll go and ask about the television set. If she took it as a bribe, then she'll splutter and protest. If a relative bought it for her or she waves a receipt at us, then we'll come back and try to find something else."

"Is this police station haunted?" said Silas.

"No, why?"

"I felt a sudden wave of cold. Mind you, I'm not used to alcohol."

"Want to lie down for a bit and I'll see Mrs. Mackenzie on my own?"

"No. I'll splash cold water on my face and I'll be fine."

CHAPTER EIGHT

Fair fa' your honest sonsie face

—Robert Burns

Women often took the bus from Cnothan to Lochdubh to shop at Patel's grocery because of his "special offers." That day it was sliced cold ham. While her mother queued up, Fairy McSporran ran along to the vet's to look at the animals. She was fascinated with the wild cat, wondering if it would ever wake up.

"Can I hae a peek?" she asked Peter, the vet.

"Aye, but don't touch anything."

Fairy darted into the back room and then stopped still, staring at the cat and all the tubes. And then the cat opened its eyes and glared at her.

She retreated backwards, her hand to her mouth, crying, "It's awake!"

The vet came rushing in. The cat lay as before, eyes closed.

"Come away, lassie. It's trick o' the light."

But the little girl seemed frightened and Peter, the vet, comforted her with a lollipop out of a jar he kept for children.

* * *

Refreshed and feeling happy again, Silas trotted along the waterfront with Hamish and the dog Lugs. Several of his colleagues back at Strathbane had sympathised with him being "banished to the backwoods." Silas thought of the awful jobs in Strathbane, mainly drugs and fights, and felt he was the luckiest policeman in the world. Hamish looked at him thoughtfully. "Not interested in anything to do with cooking or the catering business?"

"No," said Silas. "I was never allowed in the kitchen so I don't even know how to boil an egg. Why?"

"I've lost three policemen to the catering trade. That's all. Clarry is the chef at the castle, Willie of the restaurant you've met, and Dick has a bakery now in Braikie. The last one, mind you, Charlie, well that was just a combination of love and a fellow policewoman who had gone off the job as much as he had. Can we expect a visit from your mother?"

"She is trying hard but I told her it was a special assignment and if she came I would lose my job."

"Possessive, is she?"

"Very. Like I told you, she made me join the Temperance Society."

"Idle hands and all that," said Hamish thoughtfully. "Your ma needs an interest to take her mind off you. I'll find her something. So here we are at Mrs. Mackenzie's. She's gone in for gnomes, I see."

"Isn't it odd that gnomes have become fashionable again?" said Silas. "Particularly with people who like dreadful puns, like *gnome alone,* or *there's no place like gnome.* That sort of thing."

They walked up a brick path and knocked at the door. "That's odd," said Hamish. "She gives the forestry workers tea and usually she's at home now preparing it."

Few houses in Lochdubh had dinner or supper in the evenings. High tea ruled, that early meal consisting of one plate of food, ham and salad or fish-and-chips, and then bread and butter, scones, and iced cakes all washed down with strong tea.

"I saw a queue of women outside Patel's," said Silas. "Maybe she's there."

"Oh, o' course. It's cold ham day. Cold ham for tea is the caviar o' Lochdubh."

They strolled back, but there was no sign of Mrs. Mackenzie, and none of the women had seen her.

Hamish was suddenly assailed with a feeling of dread. "Let's get back there. If no one answers the door, we'll wait for the forestry workers."

Again, when they knocked and rang the bell, there was no reply. "Let's try the fire escape," said Hamish.

They walked round and into the square of weedy garden. Hamish looked up. The fire escape door was open.

He ran up the stairs, muttering, "Oh, God, no," with Silas at his heels. They ran along the corridor and hurtled down the stairs, crashing into Mrs. Mackenzie's parlour. She swung round and shouted, "What do you think you are doing?"

"Your fire escape door is standing open," said Hamish.

"And so it is. There's been a bit o' damp up there and I'm letting the breeze in."

So much for the great detective showing off his abilities to his policeman, thought Hamish gloomily.

"It is these murders," said Hamish, "and the murder of Alison. I was nervous about you. Did you know any men calling on her?"

"No, and as I've told the police over and over again until I'm sick of it, I don't allow gentlemen callers anywhere in the house except the back parlour. But no one even called on the lassie. She was a bit o' a flibbertigibbet but she always paid her rent on time."

"That's a really big television," said Silas. "Takes up most of your wall."

"Yes, my eyes aren't too good, so it is the great comfort. I havenae seen you before, young man."

"I'm Silas Dunbar, Mr. Macbeth's new policeman."

"Aye, well, the lazy loon could do wi' some help afore we all get murdered in our beds."

A streak of highland malice gripped Hamish. "Business must be good to afford a television set like that."

"It is more a case of God being good."

"Oh, really? Prayed, did you, and he sent it to land on your doorstep?"

"Don't be blasphemous or he will strike you dead, Hamish Macbeth, and the little demons in hell will stick their pitchforks in you and well you'll deserve it. The kirk in Strathbane was holding a raffle for the children of the Sudan and the first prize was that telly donated by that sheik who bought old Urquhart's castle ower near Moy Hall. I was down in Strathbane and they were selling tickets in Harold's fishmongers, he had a special on coley. I bought two tickets, even though they were a pound each. I could hardly believe it when they phoned me. It was in the papers with my photo. See!"

She pointed to the wall by the window. Sure enough, there was a newspaper photo of her receiving a huge beribboned box. Alongside her was the provost and a small man in Arab dress.

Hamish felt sulky and angry. He had just demonstrated to his new policeman that he should have known about that television set as it had been in the newspapers and no doubt the hot topic of gossip in Lochdubh.

"You should keep a better eye on what's going on here," he said. "I mean this isn't the first time that fire door has been used by a criminal."

"I cannae be everywhere at once, can I? I keep a decent house here."

"What about phone calls?"

"They've all got mobiles. Nobody uses the landline any more. Now off with you and use the front door. I won't have you pair trekking dirt through the house."

* * *

"Well, so much for one of my great ideas," said Hamish when they were outside.

"Don't worry, sir," said Silas, taking a grateful breath of pure highland air. "You've got to fantasise and theorise to solve anything. I mean, we're old-fashioned. We don't have forensics or DNA at our fingertips. We have to go through headquarters to get those, and I bet if you try they fob you off."

Hamish's bad mood evaporated. "What a comforting sort of copper you are. I'm just going to look at my cat."

They walked towards the vet's while Hamish described the rescue of Sonsie and how no one was to know he had a wild cat.

His heart sank when he saw the cat, still to all intents and purpose in a coma.

"Back to the notes," said Hamish. "There must be something we've missed."

"I've got the names of the forestry workers who assaulted him," said Silas. "If you like, I'll go back to Mrs. Mackenzie's and have a go at them."

"That would be grand. I'll see you back at the station."

Hamish looked down and found Lugs at his heels. The

dog always disappeared when he went to the vet's. He sat down in the office and pulled the large sheaf of notes towards him and then stared vacantly at the wall. There was something in Mrs. Mackenzie's conversation about that television that irked his brain, but he couldn't think what it was.

He shook his head to clear it. He could hear Lugs in the kitchen, banging his metal food bowl on the floor, and went to give him some hard dog food because he knew that Lugs had been in the kitchen of the Italian restaurant and had probably had a large meal already.

He made himself a cup of strong coffee and then lit the stove because the evenings were getting cold although it was still not the end of August. He was reluctant to go back to work but at last he dragged himself to the office. So many people had motives to want Paul English dead. It couldn't be Maggie Dinwiddy or her daughter, Holly Bates, no doubt waiting trial in America. They had been out of the country at that time. There was Caro Fleming, so cruelly tricked. The woman in Crask he had bankrupted. So very many people must have hated him with a passion. But one was around, the murderer, and that murderer must have been blackmailed by Alison. Alison lived in a fantasy world. She probably thought that Paul English deserved it and there was no harm in getting a bit of money to keep her in the heavy scent she liked and the sequinned clothes she wore off-duty. The sad fact, thought Hamish, was that if the murderer now felt secure, then there would be no more deaths—but then the murders would never be solved.

Silas came back an hour later. "They were pretty open about it. English was a bit drunk and hearing Glasgow accents started to sneer about that city, so they took him outside to throw him in the harbour. You broke it up and handcuffed English. The workers had run off. But they didn't go back or anything like that. Two of the other workers at Mrs. Mackenzie's heard her shouting at them for making a noise when they came in and giving them a lecture on temperance. So that's out of the way."

Hamish sighed. "You'd better phone Blair. He'll like to hear about the failure. See if he's got anything. I'll talk to Jimmy."

* * *

Jimmy reported that no one had ever seen Blair work so hard. In fact, too hard. A woman called Caro Fleming had complained about police harassment. Blair had gone as far as to arrest her for the murder of Paul English, have her brought in for questioning, and grill her so hard that it was only when she fainted and a doctor sent for that the full enormity of what Blair had done reached Daviot's ears and Caro had to be placated with apologies and offers of generous compensation.

"Well, he's planted Silas Dunbar to spy on me," said Hamish, "but Silas is a grand wee chap and put me wise to it. Think o' something, Jimmy. It's enough to drive a man mad."

"I don't think we're going to break this one, Hamish, and that's a fact. I've looked and looked at all the CCTV stuff and there's nothing there. There's that shadowy figure you pointed out, but it's only a darker shadow in the shadows and no idea that it's the murderer. The trouble is that the hospital is short-staffed and pretty empty at night. It really looks as if Larry will pull through, but Daviot's feeling desperate. Police Scotland are angry at all this unsolved mayhem and threatening to send some heavy guns up from Glasgow. Have you any whisky?"

"I think there's some o' the Japanese stuff, if you left any."

"That'll do," said Jimmy, opening the kitchen door and walking in. He was followed by Silas.

Hamish poured three shots of whisky and gave one to Silas. "Take that into the office and spend an hour with the notes," he said. "Then I'll make us some supper."

Silas went off. He raised the glass to his lips and then froze as he heard his mother's voice at the kitchen door. Hamish quickly slammed the office door as he passed and then Silas heard him say, "Really, Mrs. Dunbar, your son is a grown man and on duty and if you persist in following him around, then I will need to report it and he will lose his job. Do I make myself clear?"

Low-key apologies and Silas breathed a sigh of relief as he heard his mother retreat. He gulped down some whisky. It tasted awful. But a minute later he felt a warm glow. I hope I'm not becoming a dipsomaniac, he thought guiltily. But Blair had been bullying and his mother had always been bullying and he wanted to hang on to this to-hell-with-the lot-of-them feeling and so he drank the rest of the whisky and, mindful of his job, began to study the notes. He desperately wanted to find something, anything.

He finally heard Jimmy leaving, and then Hamish opened the door and came in. "I don't think your ma will be around again. Has she any friends?"

"Oh, yes, usually she's out at the church events all week."

"As long as she's not lonely."

"No, she won't be back. I heard what you said and the idea of me losing my job means loss of face and she couldn't bear that. Dad died ten years ago and she went to the kirk for comfort and it somehow got the hold of her. But it keeps her busy and happy."

"I can't be bothered cooking. I phoned my old sidekick, Dick, and he's got bacon baps. We can have those and maybe call at the hospital afterwards."

* * *

Dick Fraser, to everyone's astonishment, had married the glamorous Anka, a dazzling Polish redhead who nonetheless shared Dick's passion for baking. Their baps were famous and they did a successful business online as well as in the shop.

Silas, seated in a comfortable armchair by the peat fire in their upstairs living room above the shop, with a bacon bap in one hand and an excellent cup of coffee in the other, wished with all his heart that he could keep this job as long as possible.

Hamish had been telling Dick all about the case. "I think it's some lucky amateur, silencing people as he goes along," said Dick. "And someone, funnily enough, not scary. I mean someone who could say, 'Well, he hurt you, too, and he had it coming to him,' sort of thing. Maybe even a sort of personality you might want to protect. Sort of person who says, 'I did it for you as well as for myself.'"

"That's a thought," said Hamish, "but it'll make it all the harder to find. The only people before nasty enough were Maggie Dinwiddy and her daughter, but old Granny was off busy blackmailing someone else."

"Are you absolutely sure these forestry workers are in the clear?" asked Dick.

"Yes, Silas cleared that lot up once and for all."

"English was stabbed with a broad blade like a sword," said Dick. "Anything there?"

"Not that can be found," said Hamish. "You can still buy all sorts of swords at car boot sales and at auctions. Somewhere in these notes that I've been going over and over, there's a weak spot. I swear there's something I'm missing."

Anka came in carrying a tray of desserts. "You must try these," she said. "It's fresh strawberries, jelly and fresh cream, crushed meringue, and with just a dash of kümmel."

"This is delicious. But how much are you charging? Liqueur like kümmel is expensive."

"Not really. There's less than half a teaspoon in each one.

We charge quite a lot. Four pounds and fifty pence and yet they fly out of the shop. We're going to take some goodies up to Larry at the hospital when he's up to eating proper food again. I gather he's still not up for questioning yet?"

"Not that I've heard," said Hamish. "I don't think he'll really be able to tell us anything. Some idiot of a nurse passed him earlier and said he was asleep and she didn't like to wake him. He probably didn't see a thing."

"What about forensics?"

"Nothing. Wore gloves and, what's more, wore some sort of forensic suit."

"Could be one of you lot. Blair still crazy?"

"No. Clean and sober. But cracks are beginning to show. He's determined to find the murderer and so he's turned to his old methods of bullying people and getting into trouble. It won't be long now before we get some heavy mob up from Glasgow."

* * *

Reluctant as they were to leave the bakery, Hamish and Silas went out into the deserted evening streets of Braikie. "It seems a shame to spoil such a visit with work," said Hamish. "Let's go to the hospital and see if by some miracle any of the night staff remembers anything."

But although they diligently questioned everyone who had been on duty on both the nights—the first attempt on Alison's life and then the successful one—there seemed to be nothing new. Silas reflected that this was what was known as real police work, grinding boredom, asking the same questions over and over again. No wonder they call us plods, he thought.

"Yes, I know," said Hamish, as if Silas had spoken his thought aloud. "But there's nothing else to do but go over and go over until something breaks."

But when they returned to the station, there was something that drove every other thought out of Hamish's mind. There was a message on the office phone from the vet: "Your cat has made a miracle recovery."

Leaving Silas behind, Hamish pounded along to the vet's. "It's a real miracle," said Peter. The large cat was free of tubes and wide awake. It lazily regarded Hamish and gave a slow rumbling purr.

"Never seen anything like it," marvelled Peter. "But Hamish, I've treated Sonsie in the past and I swear this isn't Sonsie."

"I know my own cat," said Hamish, "and I'll take her now."

He gently lifted the large cat. Its rumbling purrs reverberated through him.

Lugs was waiting outside. "Here she is!" cried Hamish, but Lugs ran away, scampering in front of them until he reached the police station. When Hamish entered, Lugs was hiding under the kitchen table.

"You silly dog," said Hamish. "Don't you even recognise your old friend?"

Silas came out of the living room. The cat eyed him balefully and Silas felt a superstitious frisson of fear. "Glad you got your cat back, Hamish," he said. "I'm just going to take a walk before bedtime."

Silas went out into the cool calm of the evening. He saw a gnarled little man wearing a tight tweed jacket, sitting on the harbour wall, rolling a cigarette.

"Ower here, son," he called. Silas went to join him. "I'm Archie Maclean," he said. "You're Hamish's new copper?"

"Yes, I'm Silas Dunbar."

"Was that Sonsie I saw him bringing home?"

"His cat's made some sort of miraculous recovery."

"I used to give Sonsie a bit o' fish. I've nothing but coley and I don't know how folk can eat that. We used to throw the damn things back. Now the fish-and-chip shops try to pass it off as cod."

"What's up with it?"

"Oily, that's what. I was thinking o' going to the pub. Fancy a wee dram?"

Silas hesitated only a minute. One could do no harm. He would not admit to himself that the cat had scared him and that he was reluctant to return.

He spent a pleasant time in the pub but then decided two drinks were enough. Somewhere at the back of his mind was a feeling that something important had been said and it was something he ought to tell Hamish. But Hamish had gone to bed, and no doubt the cat had gone with him. He went into his own bedroom after undressing and washing. He was just climbing in when the door was nudged open and

Lugs came in and jumped up on the bed. "No you don't," said Silas, trying to push the dog off, but that was when he realised Lugs was trembling. "There, now," said Silas. "You can stay. Did the cat frighten you?" He patted and hugged Lugs until the animal stretched out beside him on the bed, heaved a little sigh, and fell asleep.

"Can't blame you," was Silas's last remark. "That damn cat scares me as well."

* * *

The following weekend, late in the evening, Priscilla Halburton-Smythe arrived at the hotel and found that Elspeth Grant was one of the guests. The two met in reception. "Been to see Hamish yet?" asked Priscilla. She had heard all the rumours about Hamish having had an affair with Elspeth but did not want to believe it.

"Not yet. In fact, I was just on my way. I hear he's got his wife back."

"What wife?"

"Sonsie. I think he's tied closer to that animal than to any woman."

"I'll come with you," said Priscilla. "I rather liked Sonsie. But isn't it a bit late for a visit?"

"If he's asleep, the bedroom door will be closed and we can just walk away."

They entered quietly by the kitchen door. The bedroom door was open. "Must be in the living room," said Elspeth.

They stood in the doorway of the living room. Hamish was asleep on the sofa. On his lap was the large cat. As they stood at the entrance to the room, the cat slowly turned its large head, stretched up one large paw possessively on Hamish's chest, and gave them both a yellow stare of such malignance that Elspeth gasped and drew Priscilla away.

Outside, Elspeth, her odd silver eyes gleaming in the twilight, said, "I don't know what Hamish brought in from the moor but it's evil and it's not Sonsie."

"You must tell him!" said Priscilla.

"He won't listen to me. The only thing that's going to get rid of that creature is a silver bullet!"

CHAPTER NINE

I would like to be there, were it but to see the way the cat jumps.

—Sir Walter Scott

To Silas's relief, Sonsie would not get into the police Land Rover. To go off with Hamish and Lugs, leaving that sinister beast behind, gave him a feeling of reprieve. There had initially been many visitors, but they soon found out that Hamish would not listen to any remarks about the cat not looking like Sonsie. Even his friend Angela Brodie said sadly to her husband that she thought Hamish was bewitched.

Also to Silas's relief, Blair had stopped calling, demanding results. So the days of cruising around Hamish's extensive beat were relaxed and pleasant.

One day when they had been fishing on the River Anstey and caught four trout, Hamish said, "Well, that's one each and two for Sonsie. They are not getting much out of the loch these days, mostly things like mackerel and coley, and I cannae stand coley."

Something tugged at Silas's memory. "I've got something!" he cried.

"Doesnae seem to be anything on your line," said Hamish.

"Not that! Mrs. Mackenzie. Don't you remember? She said she had gone all the way to Strathbane because Harold, the fishmonger, had a special on coley. That's how she got tickets for the raffle and won that television. But why go all that way and pay the expense of the bus fare to buy a type of fish that Archie might have given her for nothing?"

"You mean, could the raffle have been rigged?"

"Something like that."

"What are the reports on this sheik?"

"Highly respectable. Bought Ferry Castle from the Urquhart family. Long name but shortened locally to Sheik Khalid al-Faher. Comes for the shooting every August but usually stays on until the end of the year. Contributes a lot to local charities. I see you've got a silver cup in your living room that you won at a clay pigeon shoot. Well, I saw in the paper that there's one at the sheik's this Saturday. Let's see if there's time to put your name down. See, he'll probably award the prize, and if you win maybe you could be having a wee word."

"If he's all that respectable, how could he have rigged the prize?"

"I don't know," fretted Silas. "But we've got nothing else."

* * *

They hurried back to the station. After various phone calls, they found there was still time to enter, but the fee was fifty-nine pounds, ninety-nine pence. "Why can't they just say sixty pounds and be done with it," complained Hamish. "Hey! Where's Sonsie? Got some nice trout. Where are you?"

But there was no sign of the cat. Hamish slumped down in an armchair and looked bleakly around. "Now what do I do?" he asked.

"Just wait," said Silas. "It'll be back."

Before Saturday, Silas suggested that Hamish might like to get some practice in, but Hamish was afraid that if Sonsie came back the sound of his gun might frighten her away.

* * *

When they drove down to Ferry Castle on the Saturday, Hamish began to feel silly. It was all too far-fetched. It would have been cheaper to simply ask Mrs. Mackenzie about the peculiar lure of cheap coley and see if that made her look guilty. He brightened when he learned there was not only a trophy but a cash prize of one thousand pounds, for he still owed the vet money for Sonsie's treatment, the money from the fund-raising having quickly disappeared. He glanced at the competition and recognised two crack shots up from Glasgow and began to wish he had practised.

But when he started shooting, it seemed as if his eyes had never been so sharp or his aim so accurate.

Silas joined in the loud cheers as Hamish went up to the rostrum to collect his prize. But it was being given by Lord Samson, an industrial bigwig, surrounded by the worthies of Strathbane. "I would have liked to thank the sheik himself," said Hamish.

"He's down in London. He would have loved your performance. Never seen shooting like it."

"Now what?" asked Hamish when he joined Silas. "I cannae complain it's been a waste o' time, because I need the money."

"I remember now," said Silas. "It was the kirk running the charity raffle. Probably that big Church of Scotland in Strathbane. My mother goes there. We'll drop in on her. Maybe we might get Lugs a wee treat. He's a grand dog."

"Funny how he and Sonsie used to be almost inseparable," said Hamish.

"Well, like I said, the general opinion in Lochdubh is that you want that cat so much to be Sonsie, you've become blind to the fact that it isn't."

"Bad injuries and ill treatment change people's characters," protested Hamish. "Animals as well."

"But I found some photos o' Sonsie. She looks a wee bit smaller and the markings are lighter."

"I'll have a proper look when I get back," said Hamish. "They say love is blind and I really do love that cat."

"That cat, whatever it is, is not lovable, sir. It scares the pants off me. Here we are. That wee bungalow."

It was a pebble-dashed building. The garden in front had been paved over and nothing planted. A fairly new Subaru was parked outside the front door.

Mrs. Dunbar opened the door before they could ring the bell. She was a round woman with a dumpy figure wrapped in a cardigan and a long tweed skirt. Her face was round as well with faded-blue eyes and a button of a nose. Her hair was thin and wispy.

"This is a treat," she cried. "Come ben and I'll put the kettle on."

Silas and Hamish followed into a small kitchen. "It's like this," said Hamish. "There was the grand prize of a big television set to be won in a raffle funded by the local sheik. Was there any chance that the lady who won it was told to buy tickets? That in some way she might have been selected?"

"Oh, the kirk would never do that!" Mrs. Dunbar looked genuinely shocked. "But as my wee boy is a policeman now, I'd better hae a hard think." She deftly tipped boiling water into a teapot and then proceeded to load a tray with all the things she considered necessary for afternoon tea.

"I hope you are taking good care of my boy, Sergeant."

"Like a father," said Hamish solemnly.

"I must say I never thought that the police could be so caring. Thank you, Sergeant," she added as Hamish relieved her of the heavy tray. "Follow me."

The living room contained the usual three-piece suite although this one was covered in frilly cushions and fake silk throws of an acid-pink colour. There was a copy of Landseer's *Stag at Bay* over the empty fireplace and photos in silver frames of Silas at various ages on top of an upright piano. As instructed, Hamish put the tea tray down on a coffee table and they all sat around it.

"The only thing," said Mrs. Dunbar, "was about a month before the raffle was drawn, I was asked if I knew anyone worthy who deserved it. You know, a regular kirk member. I think the elders were beginning to be worried that such a prize should end up in the hands of some lowlife. I'll give you the phone numbers of two of our elders and you can ask them. Now, fairy cakes, anyone?"

* * *

Once back in the police Land Rover, Hamish felt a little pang of guilt that Silas had brought two biscuits for Lugs. He felt he had been neglecting the dog for a long time. When he entered the police station, he knew immediately that the cat was missing. He had to admit to himself that when the cat was there, there was always an atmosphere of threat.

He went up and down the village calling for the cat. He asked around but no one had seen it. He called at the vet's but Peter had not seen the cat. "Tell me, Peter," said Hamish, "did you ever think the cat might not be Sonsie?"

"All the time. I tried to tell you, but you were so determined that cat was Sonsie, you wouldn't listen. Don't go rushing back to Ardnamurchan, Hamish. Sonsie's in her proper place. And the other cat must have returned to the wild where it belongs."

Silas was surprised when Hamish showed every sign of pursuing the Mrs. Mackenzie angle. To even suggest the Church of Scotland had rigged the raffle amounted in his mind to sacrilege. The first elder he phoned, a Mr. Witherspoon, answered mildly enough that he had never been asked to suggest anyone and the idea was ridiculous. Such a great man as the sheik or any of his aides would not trouble themselves over fixing a raffle. The next elder, a Mr. Noble, immediately flew into a temper and threatened to report Hamish to his superiors. Hamish eventually managed to soothe him because any report to his superiors could mean Blair getting hold of this line of enquiry.

There must be something in it, he thought. I mean, why would a woman go all the way to Strathbane to buy two cheap fish?

Well, the simple way was just to go and ask her. Mr. Mackenzie answered the door to him and then stalked in front of him into her private parlour, where the large television set was showing the umpteenth episode of an Australian soap. "It's only got a few minutes to go," Mrs. Mackenzie shouted above the noise from the set. "You'll have to wait."

Someone on the screen was in a coma in hospital. Hamish reflected that when soap operas felt they were running out of plot, they always put one of their characters in a coma and someone at the bedside was always being told, "Do talk. She can hear you."

When it finished, Mrs. Mackenzie turned the sound down but left the picture on. Little coloured lights from the screen flickered across her thick glasses.

"Why did you go all the way to Strathbane to buy coley?" asked Hamish. "I mean, it's possible Archie would ha' given you a couple for nothing, and Patel sells them cheap."

She turned and addressed the television set. "I just happened to be in Strathbane, that's all. I often go on a Saturday."

"The buses are expensive these days."

"Not for me. I'm an old-age pensioner and I've got a free bus pass."

"You go to the kirk there rather than here?"

"Not all of the time."

"Do you often buy raffle tickets?"

"Why all these questions? If you must know, I was waiting for the bus when Mr. Alexander drove up and asked me if I would like a lift. I says, says I, 'That would be real kind,' because often the bus is late. He dropped me at the fishmonger's shop and he says to me, 'He's selling raffle tickets. You should have a flutter.' I was that amazed because Mr. Alexander is an elder o' the kirk. Well, I didnae like just to ask which is why I bought the coley first. But Mr. Alexander fair urged me and he waited until I had bought the tickets."

Hamish studied her and Mrs. Mackenzie studied the floor. That was nearly the truth, thought Hamish, but there's something she's not telling me. On the wall was a piece of embroidery in a wooden frame bearing the legend HIS EYE IS ON THE SPARROW.

Hamish pointed at it. "Believe that, do you? That he knows everything we say and do?"

"Yes."

"Does he know when we are lying?"

"What is this? Yes, if you must know."

"Not telling the whole truth is a form of lying, wouldn't you say?"

She suddenly went into a rage. "Get out o' here. I don't need to answer stupid questions. Out!"

Outside, Hamish knew he should try to find this Mr. Alexander, but he longed to spend the day looking for his cat. Yes, he finally admitted, he had probably made a mistake, the cat might not be Sonsie but she could be injured. He could send Silas but it was getting late and Silas was so in awe of the church that he wouldn't really press this Mr. Alexander.

He decided to go back to his notes and try to find Mr. Alexander in the morning. He was pleased to find that Silas had already found a phone number and address for the elder which he had got from the Lochdubh minister, Mr. Wellington. So Hamish walked up the moors at the back of the station, whistling for the cat the way he used to whistle for Sonsie. But nothing disturbed the calmness of the evening. He walked sadly back indoors. He had wasted emotion, time, and money under the delusion that he had found Sonsie again. He felt almost as if he had been bewitched. The villagers had been frightened of the cat, and Elspeth had left a message for him saying she could not visit him until he got rid of the animal.

The clay pigeon prize money paid the rest of the vet's bill with a third left over, so Hamish suggested they go to the Italian restaurant and treat themselves.

"I've been thinking," said Silas, "that I should tell Mr. Blair I will not spy on you, and if he insists I will need to report him."

"Don't do that," said Hamish quickly. "I think Blair is still not quite right in the head and can be dangerous. Just feed him a bit here and there. He thinks I'm stupid most of the time so he won't be all that surprised. He thinks I solve cases by sheer luck, that's all. I mean, I could be wasting time and effort thinking that Mrs. Mackenzie knows something and was being bribed in a complicated way. But I've got nothing else. I mean, the woman is famous for spying on her boarders. If she didn't have such cheap rates, she wouldn't have anyone at all."

"Maybe it could have been like this," said Silas. "They want to make a big show of the presentation. What if it's won by some criminal or blowsy slag from those tower blocks by the docks? Won't look good in the papers. They decided to massage it a bit. Get someone worthy to win it, someone outside Strathbane. So they hit on Mrs. Mackenzie."

"Could have gone wrong. Mrs. Mackenzie is the kind

who might think buying a raffle ticket was gambling and a fast track to hell. I'll know better when I meet this Mr. Alexander."

* * *

Silas woke suddenly during the night with a feeling of dread. The door of his bedroom was nudged open and then Lugs jumped on his bed and lay trembling beside him. There seemed to be an air of menace enveloping the station. And then it was gone.

That damn cat, thought Silas. It hasn't left. It's lurking around somewhere.

* * *

Mr. Jonathan Alexander, a retired coal merchant, lived up on the moors outside Strathbane in a granite stone villa on a windy hilltop. He was at home and ushered them into a cold living room where little icy draughts scuttled across the stone floor, covered only in a hooked rug. The walls held bookshelves full of dark leather-bound tomes. One small paned window rattled in the gale.

He was a tall, knobbly sort of man. His cadaverous face had two knobs above his pale grey eyes, and his large hands were knobbly with arthritis.

Hamish's curiosity overcame him. "Why build your house up on the hill where there's no shelter?"

"That was my father's doing. He always was a silly old fool," said Mr. Alexander with surprising viciousness from one who was supposed to be a Christian. "So what brings the police to my humble abode? I could be of help to you. I was in the Black Watch for my sins."

The man's a walking cliché, thought Hamish.

"A Mrs. Mackenzie won an expensive television set in a raffle."

"Oh, aye? And what would that be doing wi' me?"

"As it was for a worthy cause and the TV was very expensive, we wondered if there was any way that the winner could have been chosen?"

"Well, don't ask me. I just do all the work while the rest o' the worthies ponce about."

"But is it possible?"

"Naw. Daft idea. Too complicated."

He had begun to look almost truculent. "Look, laddie. My corns hurt and I want ma tea. Bugger off."

"So that's that," said Hamish back at the station. "It was just a mad idea of mine. You know, in books it's always the one you'd least suspect, whereas in real life it's usually the obvious one."

"Who's that, sir?"

"As you're not cheeky, you can call me Hamish. Oh, whatsername? The minister at Cnothan."

"But I've gone over and over the interviews. You weren't the only one. Jimmy Anderson and Blair both interviewed her. On the night of English's murder and at the estimated time, she was seen by passing villagers in the manse, in her study, working at her desk."

"Oh, I tried to find a way around it. I mean, that wee lassie, McSporran, was telling the truth about the 'carnival' knowledge as she called it. So, I thought, English was always after money. He had his wicked way with her. What if she told him she's left it all to charity instead of him. Sort of a test of his true love and all that. He gives her the heave-ho in his usual charming way and she turns murderous."

The wind rose suddenly and moaned round the station. Silas shivered. "I feel that cat's somewhere near."

"I'll go out and look for the poor thing," said Hamish. "Come on, Lugs."

But Lugs shuffled over to Silas, laid his chin on Silas's boots, and looked pleadingly at Hamish.

"Oh, stay where you are, you stupid dog. Could you cook us a fry-up for supper, Silas? There's venison sausage, eggs, bacon, and haggis."

"Will do. Do you want me to report that business about the minister to Blair? Send him down the wrong rabbit hole?"

"That's a good idea."

* * *

Blair said he would check the interviews and get back to Silas which he did after ten minutes, calling Silas every sort of fool. The woman had an unbreakable alibi which Silas should have known if he had a brain in his body and on and on went Blair until Silas said firmly that somehow Hamish was sure Maisie Walters was the murderer. After he had rung off, Blair stared at the phone, overcome by a sudden craving for a drink. He had run out of pills and had taken no mind-bending substances. Drugs were dangerous, he told himself. But what harm could just one dram do? He needed to think. Silas was young and naive. He wouldn't lie. Despite all appearances to the contrary, Macbeth might be onto something.

He set out for Cnothan. Maisie Walters herself answered the door to him, her face darkening when she saw who it was. Blair gave her an oily smile and said, "I'm only here because it baffles me why Hamish Macbeth should think you are the murderer."

"Tell Macbeth I am contacting my lawyer this evening and I am going to sue him."

Blair felt alarmed. He could not produce proof because that would mean admitting he had asked Silas to spy on Macbeth. "I havenae any proof he's actually saying that," blustered Blair. "Just a rumour."

"Then either get proof and come back with it or go away before I report you for police harassment."

* * *

Blair was furious when he left the manse. He drove to Lochdubh and parked on the waterfront. He decided to creep round the back of the station and listen at the kitchen window. He couldn't bear the idea of a wasted journey. The craving for drink was worse than ever.

As he tiptoed to the side of the station, he heard a loud hiss and looked down. A large cat with a dead hen in its jaws was staring up at him with a yellow, baleful stare. It dropped the hen and Blair could swear it was ready to leap on him. He turned and ran for his car.

* * *

"Did you hear anything?" asked Hamish, putting down his knife and fork.

"No, but I feel something. I think your cat's about the place."

"I searched and called while you were making supper," said Hamish.

"What on earth made you think it was your cat? Everyone in the village is saying it wasn't in the least like Sonsie."

"I wanted it to be. And I have a feeling she wanted to be, too. Is that mad?"

"I suppose it could be," said Silas cautiously. "What do you think Blair will do?"

"He may try to get something out of her and fail and that'll make him mad. If he goes back on the booze, that's when you're really in trouble. He'll maybe persuade Daviot that you'd be better off in Strathbane. Next time you call, you'd better tell him you hate it here."

* * *

A report of a break-in at a shop in Braikie kept them busy the next morning. Silas said he would do the paperwork and Hamish decided to drive to Cnothan, just to question one of the witnesses. Perhaps they might have been lying.

How he detested Cnothan! A sour village where the inhabitants boasted of "keeping themselves to themselves." There used to be a Sergeant Macgregor to cope with the place, but he had retired and it had simply been added on to Hamish's extensive beat. The witness, a George Green, actually lived in what had been Sergeant Macgregor's bungalow. The front garden was packed with the dreariest bunch of plants Hamish had ever seen in one small garden. He recognised laurel bushes and wellingtonia. The rest he didn't know but they were flowerless and dusty and depressing. He was just about to walk up the garden path when the sound of a small sob stopped him.

He unclipped the torch from his belt and shone it into the foliage from which the sound had come.

The terrified eyes of Fairy McSporran stared up at him.

CHAPTER TEN

I believe cats to be spirits come to earth.

—Jules Verne

Hamish crouched down. "It's me. Sergeant Macbeth. What's the matter, lassie?"

She put her hands over her face and began to rock to and fro. "I'd best get you home," said Hamish, becoming alarmed.

"No!" she screamed. "Ma will say I'm telling lies and the minister will put a curse on me. She can be two places at the one time."

"Come with me, lassie. I think what you need is a chocolate ice cream."

"Wi' a chocolate flake in it?"

"Double, if ye want it."

One small grubby hand reached out from the bushes and found Hamish's hand and held on tightly. He lifted her up in his arms and walked down to a café on the main street where he bought her something called a 99, which came with a stick of flaky chocolate thrust into the cone, and asked for another flake. Oh, the magic of chocolate, thought Hamish, watching the delight on the tearstained face. Better than a tranquilliser any day.

"We'll talk a wee bit about what scared you. Now, Fairy, I'm sure you believe what you think you saw but folk cannae be two places at once."

She looked at him solemnly. "I saw her at the Girl Guides. She needed some string so she says to me to go into the vestry and look in the green cupboard and there might be some on the bottom shelf. Mr. Macbeth, cross ma hert and hope to die but when I opened that door, she's there, looking at me. I ran like hell and hid."

"Listen, Fairy, I believe you, but it is our secret, right? Can you keep quiet for, say, a couple of days and...and I'll buy you another 99?"

"Another 99 and I can shut up for a year," said Fairy.

"Right. When you've finished the next ice cream, I'll take you near your home and drop you off. Is the church locked during the day?"

She shook her head. He bought her another ice cream and waited patiently, very patiently, because Fairy, having got over her fears, seemed determined to make it last as long as possible.

When he had at last got rid of her, he went up to the church, entered the vestry, and opened the green cupboard.

There was nothing sinister there, only rusty tools, and boxes of string and tape. Was Fairy nothing more than a fantasist, telling elaborate lies? But she *had* been very frightened.

He tried the other cupboards. Only the minister's robes along with the choir's surplices. Rather high even for the Church of Scotland, thought Hamish. He was about to leave when he sniffed the air and smelled smoke. He went out and looked at the sky. A thin plume of smoke was coming from the vicarage garden at the back of the manse. He ran round and vaulted over the fence, as the gate was padlocked. A brazier was burning brightly over by the far wall. He ran up to it. There was one piece of cardboard which he jerked out by using a branch. One colour-photographed eye stared up at him. That was it, he thought. Fairy had seen a large cardboard photo of the minister in the cupboard, because he recognised her even from the small piece that was left. His heart began to beat with excitement. Say Maisie left a large cardboard cutout of herself by the window on the night Paul was murdered; that would be what the witnesses saw. But the evidence was almost gone. Fairy would be dismissed as a liar. His phone rang. It was Blair. "You're to get the hell away from that manse," he shouted. "Daviot is furious. You're trespassing without a warrant."

"I'm leaving now," said Hamish mildly. "I saw smoke and went to check, that's all."

"Well, get your scrawny arse back to Lochdubh toot sweet, and tell Silas Dunbar to move back to Strathbane next week. He's not helping up there."

Hamish's heart sank. He could hear all the sounds of a pub in the background. Blair back on the booze would be even more obstructive and vicious.

* * *

He felt depressed as he made his way back to Lochdubh. He would have been even more depressed if he had seen Fairy being dragged along in the direction of the church. But he was soon to find out the result. He had only just entered the station when he was told to report to Strathbane to answer a charge of paedophilia.

By the time he had untangled the charges against him, he felt exhausted. Fairy, desperate to keep their secret, had agreed that Hamish had taken her for two ice creams and, yes, he had put a hand on her knee. Fortunately for Hamish, the waitress, like the late Paul English, prided herself on her honesty and said roundly that Hamish had never touched the wee lassie. Before he left, she had asked the officer what was up with the wee girl and he had said she was worried about schoolwork. Faced with this, Fairy had hung her head and said it was the truth but that she hadn't wanted her mother to know she was worried about school. Finally released after signing what seemed like endless statements, Hamish finally returned to Lochdubh to find a distressed Silas, who had received an e-mail summoning him back to his duties in Strathbane. Hamish had forgotten to tell him about Blair's call. He went to bed, vowing to find some way of keeping young Silas and, more important, to find evidence of those cardboard photos or photo. They must have been used at some time for something. Just before he went to sleep, he remembered that the Currie sisters sometimes went to services in Cnothan. He became determined to question them in the morning.

* * *

Silas decided that if he really had to go back to Strathbane then he would resign from the police force, or maybe, just maybe, get a transfer to a pleasant town like Perth. He quailed at the thought of living with his domineering and possessive mother again while at work he suffered the lash of Blair bullying. Hamish told him after a phone call from Jimmy that two top detectives had been sent up from Glasgow to take over running the case and Blair looked as if he was about to have an apoplexy. The phone rang before Hamish left the station. It was Blair demanding to speak to Silas.

"I am afraid Constable Dunbar is out on a case," said Hamish.

"Tell him to drop everything and get down here."

"As he is being moved at your request, sir, then you must fill in all the necessary forms in triplicate, giving reasons and..."

Hamish grinned as Blair slammed down the phone on him. He saw Silas watching him anxiously. "You are not, re-peat, not, going back to Strathbane, laddie, so stop looking like a ghost. I want you to go to Cnothan and start asking round if there were any cardboard cutouts of the minister at any time."

After Silas had left, Hamish strolled along the waterfront to the Currie sisters' cottage. He pinned a smile on his face as Nessie berated him for being lazy and her sister echoed her every word. When she had worn herself out, he started to question her about any big cardboard photographs of the minister. But neither of the spinster twins had seen anything like such a thing.

Over in Cnothan, Silas was meeting with the same lack of success. He phoned Hamish, who said, "Maybe it was something in her past. Maybe when she was married to yon oilman and afore she became a minister. Come back here and we'll start ferreting."

Their ferreting took them along to the offices of the local newspaper, the *Highland Times*. Hamish felt almost a pang of loss when he remembered the days when Elspeth had worked for the paper, before she became famous. Maybe he should have proposed to her then. They asked if they could search the photo files. Two thick box files contained photos of Minister Maisie, but nothing of the time before she took holy orders. Hamish's mind drifted off. Did members of the Church of Scotland take holy orders or was that considered papist, like taking orders from Rome? How little he knew about religion. But he had met many preachers who really should have gone on the stage, as his mother would say, and got it out of their systems. There was Maisie in tights, rehearsing as principal boy in the pantomime *Mother Goose.* What vanity, thought Hamish. What great fat legs and greasy hair. Odd life when plain women often thought they were Cleopatra and pretty girls thought they were plain. Of course, those thoughts would be damned as sexist these days. Hamish scowled. Women, he thought, were still being treated like some minor, not quite developed ethnic group and often given jobs they were not qualified for to fill some government quota. Women…

He shook his head as if to shake out the nasty thoughts, foreign to his usually easy-going mind. He felt almost haunted.

"Silas!" he said suddenly. "Come here and look at our reverend in all the glory of silk tights and high heels. Must be awfy vain. Listen, I'll bet she had a big photo of herself taken to put outside the church hall when the panto was on. What's the date? Just a few months ago. Not even near Christmas. Let's find the article that goes wi' this."

He disappeared and came back with a large bound book. "Would you believe it? Nothing on computer. Still bound in volumes like this one. Let's see. Who the hell is smoking? I don't think you're supposed to in here."

"It's the editor," said Silas, looking round the door.

Hamish cursed under his breath. He had given up smoking but the smell of that cigarette had brought back all the old craving.

He opened the book and began to look through the editions. "Nothing," he finally said. "But if there was a big cardboard photo of her outside where the panto was supposed to be put on or rehearsed, folk would remember it."

"I'll go to Cnothan and ask Maisie's alibi witnesses who said they saw her through the study window the night of Paul's murder."

* * *

Silas felt that if in some small way he could break the case then he would be allowed to stay in Lochdubh. He had just arrived in Cnothan when his mobile phone rang. It was Blair. "Has yon loon found out anything?"

"Aye," said Silas. "We've found out the murderer. It's the woman minister in Cnothan."

"Havers, laddie. Her alibi is rock-solid."

"There's a way around that." And desperate to show he was better placed in Lochdubh, Silas blurted out about the cardboard photo.

"Stay where you are!" barked Blair. "I'm coming over. Where are you?"

"Nearly at the manse."

"Stay near it but don't go in. Get it?"

"Yes, sir," mumbled Silas.

Silas now felt wretched. Blair would bully the minister who would complain to Daviot and the whole wrath of police headquarters would descend on Hamish Macbeth and it was all his, Silas's, fault.

He phoned Hamish and told him in faltering tones what he had done. Hamish reflected sadly that Charlie would never have made such a mistake. Silas was so young and, unfortunately, it seemed, easily intimidated.

Hamish decided to drive over to Cnothan to protect Silas. He cursed Silas's mother under his breath as he drove along, feeling that domineering lady had filleted Silas's backbone out of him. But when he drove up and around the manse there was no sign of Silas or his car. He banged on the door and harangued Maisie, who said she would complain about police harassment and that she had never seen Silas that morning.

Silas finally answered his phone. He said gloomily he couldn't take any more and that he was heading for the Tommel Castle Hotel to get drunk.

Hamish was worried that he had so much faith in a bit of burnt cardboard.

* * *

The journey to the hotel had gone a long way to calm Silas. He decided he hated police work. No, that was wrong. He hated Strathbane's idea of police work. He would hand in his resignation and maybe get a job as a security guard.

He decided to go into the hotel anyway, but for coffee instead of liquor. George Halburton-Smythe saw the uniformed policeman go into the bar. George had just arrived back from Uist. Kind as Charlie and Annie always were to him, he felt like an old gooseberry, lurking around the edges of their happiness, if, he thought sourly, gooseberries could be said to lurk. He followed Silas into the bar. "Let me get you something," said George.

He was feeling lonely. "That is very kind of you, sir," said Silas. "I will have a black coffee."

"I'll have one, too. Sit down. What brings you here?"

"I need to get my breath," said Silas miserably. "I've decided to leave the police force."

"Now, why is that? My friend Charles Carter wanted out as well."

"They want me to go back to Strathbane and I love it here. When I go back, I will be bullied by Mr. Blair."

George thought quickly. It had been handy when Charlie had been in the apartment downstairs to have a policeman on the premises and great to have someone to talk to in the evenings. George would never quite get rid of snobbery. But here was Silas, young, clean, and suitably deferential.

"Are you really sure you want to leave the force?" asked George. "Mr. Daviot is by way of being a friend of mine and I could arrange things for you."

"No," said Silas. "I've made up my mind."

"Well, here's what I think. You could get a job with me as security and take over Charlie's apartment. Good pay. Mind you, I'd expect you to patrol outside as well."

So must a tortured animal feel when it sees the trap open, thought Silas romantically.

* * *

When Hamish arrived, he was told by the manager that Silas and George were both down in Charlie's old apartment. Hamish hesitated at the top of the stairs, standing on one leg like a heron, a dazed look on his face.

"What's the matter?" asked the manager, Mr. Johnson.

"Say you wanted folk to think you were at work in the office when you were in fact at a brothel in Inverness, how would you cover your tracks?"

"Cut that oot, Hamish! I wouldnae be seen deid in a brothel," exclaimed the manager, his usually more refined vowels slipping.

"Oh, help me out here! Think."

"The classic thing," said the manager, "is what kids do. They make a dummy and put it in the bed so that if Ma looks in she'll think they're asleep."

"But you want folk to see you awake!"

"Listen. I pay taxes so you can use your brain. Not mine. You take said dummy and prop it up near the window with a dim light behind it. You take a selfie photo, profile, on the computer and print it off, glue it onto a melon or something, and stick a wig or cap on top. Something like that."

Hamish darted down the stairs to hear Silas say, "It's a right bonnie apartment, sir, and it will be a privilege to work for you."

They both turned round and saw Hamish. Silas turned red with embarrassment. "Hamish, I..."

"Never mind," said Hamish. "Sit down until I tell you this theory."

They both listened carefully. Then Silas said cautiously, "Have you considered that it might have nothing at all to do with the minister?"

"I've thought and thought," said Hamish. "Paul English could be vicious. He pressures her into writing a will. There's a thing! Strathbane got round every lawyer for miles and she never made a will. Anyway, she gets suspicious that all he wants is her money, and she's very vain. So to test his love she tells him she's leaving it to some animal charity. So he blows his top and tells her exactly what he thinks of her and I bet it was something awful. But before he leaves the pub, even though he's handcuffed, he's got her number on speed dial. Presses the button and begs. Say he says he'll meet her in the garden at Mrs. Mackenzie's. Alison sees her and Mrs. Mackenzie might have heard or seen something. Alison is flattered and seduced by English. I cannae understand it. He was an ugly bastard. But cupidity equals stupidity. Oh, well, maybe he promised to take her to Paris on honeymoon after they were married."

"If she's guilty," said Silas, "what do you think she'll do now?"

"Head for the station in Lochdubh to threaten me," said Hamish. "Something like that."

"I am leaving the force and going to work as the hotel security," said Silas.

"That's grand," said Hamish.

"Have you considered that it might be very simple," said Silas. "I mean, the forestry workers could have come back and tipped him into the bog after having stabbed him on the neck."

"The forestry workers are the type to lash out when angry but they would never nearly kill Larry or murder poor Alison. I'll leave you here, Silas, in case Blair's on the warpath."

Hamish had to confess that he felt relieved at Silas's decision. Silas was not Charlie. For despite his dislike for police work Charlie had been a very good policeman indeed, whereas Silas, although hardworking and good-natured, was not the sort to stand up to bullies. He drove up to the station and parked outside. Then he felt it—menace in the very air. Behind him Lugs let out a low whimper.

"What's the matter, boy?" whispered Hamish. "What's scared you?"

Lugs was a mixture of breeds, but somewhere in him must have been a bit of gun dog because he raised one paw and pointed with his nose in the direction of the henhouse.

Hamish walked over to the hen run outside the birds' shed and looked down on a massacre. Blood and feathers everywhere. Hens with their throats ripped out and left to die. He had kept eleven laying hens and one cock. He counted eleven bodies.

"I'll murder that fox," he muttered.

"Wasnae the fox," said a voice behind him, making him jump. Hamish swung round.

Archie Maclean stood there. "Was that cat o' yours," he said.

"Why didn't you stop her?" asked Hamish.

"If I'd even tried, I'd hae ended up like yon birds. Sonsie, be damned. That cat is evil. You're going to have to shoot it."

"I cannae dae that."

"Then phone that lot ower in Ardnamurchan and say a wild cat's been seen and get them to come and hunt for it. It's round the village. We're all locking our doors and windows tonight."

Hamish decided to leave clearing up the mess until the morning. How on earth had he believed so fiercely that this feral cat was Sonsie? It was as if he had been bewitched. Elspeth Grant used to laugh at him and say he was married to Sonsie.

Once indoors, he phoned Peter, the vet, and said he would like to borrow a couple of tranquilliser guns in the morning. When Silas arrived, he told him what had happened. Although Silas cringed at the thought of the cat, he felt obliged to help Hamish. Hamish suggested that Silas also go to Dr. Brodie and claim to have had a nervous breakdown which necessitated him leaving the force immediately; otherwise they would keep him down in Strathbane for weeks, signing form after form.

"And after we've dealt with that, let's see if we can get a search warrant for the manse."

"You'll never get one, sir!" exclaimed Silas.

"Oh, yes, I bloody well will! I know that bitch is hiding something or someone or she's the murderer. What will get you a house search? That wonderful word, *paedophilia.* Suggest there's been kiddy fiddling at the manse, anonymous calls, that sort of thing, and social services will be there like a shot. And we'll be at their heels."

* * *

The next morning was what Hamish always thought of as a silver day. Cobwebs decorated with silver pearls of moisture hung from the fences. White mist lay in long bands over the surface of the steel-grey loch. The air was very still, and sounds from far away came to Hamish's ears as they collected the guns and started the hunt. They tracked the cat up the back and over the fields to the peat stacks, stopping to examine spots of blood and bits of feather and hen skin. The last trace was one sad bloodstained beak and then there was nothing, not even a paw print, although the peat was damp.

The last thing Silas wanted was to come across that cat from hell. He was relieved when Hamish said they should leave it and go back and see if they could stir Maisie, the minister, up.

Hamish phoned Jimmy but Jimmy said Blair was over at the manse, and Maisie Walter had phoned Daviot, her local MP, the newspapers, and finally the prime minister. Blair, called back to the station and on the carpet, blamed

Silas, but Daviot had heard that Silas had suffered a nervous breakdown, due, the colonel had said, to Blair's bullying. Blair promised to leave the minister alone. That was when Hamish threw his hand grenade of suspected paedophilia into the mix. When he replaced the phone, he grinned at Silas and said, "Stand by for orders. They'll pussyfoot around a murder but they're great at getting children seized from their parents."

It was unfortunate for Maisie, who didn't have children anyway, that in these days of political correctness, you dare not even pat a child on the head. Mothers remembered uneasily how the minister had hugged little Johnny when he had fallen in a game of rounders, or how little Jane had been carried by the minister into the vestry to get her grazed knee treated but the door had been shut in her mother's face, and what went on in there. Hey?

But in an interview that evening on television, Maisie made a powerful speech in her defence and then burst into tears. Phone calls of support came from all over. Finally, the blame fell on Silas. It was explained that a young policeman suffering from a nervous breakdown had made a terrible mistake. Compensation would be paid along with full apologies.

"This is terrible," Silas said later to Hamish. "With all that on my record, if I don't like it at the hotel, or they don't like me, I'll never get another job."

"Don't worry. I'll wipe it off your record."

"How?"

"I have my methods, Watson. Don't ask. The vet wants the guns back."

Silas reluctantly handed his over. He had planned to sleep with it beside the bed.

Lugs slept beside Silas. It was almost as if the dog feared that if he went back to sleeping with Hamish, then the cat might find him.

Before Hamish fell asleep, he had a phone call from Charlie and told him about the massacre of the hens. "I'll come over tomorrow with my gun," said Charlie, "and blast that bugger off the face o' the earth."

"No, I'll deal with it," said Hamish.

"What the hell made you think thon beastie was Sonsie?" asked Charlie.

"I don't know."

"Well, I do," said Charlie. "There are things out on those moors and mountains that belong in hell, that's what."

"Aw, come off it. That's superstitious rubbish."

"Oh, yeah? So how come you got tricked into thinking that was your cat?"

"I haven't the faintest idea," shouted Hamish. "Sorry. I'll call you later."

* * *

The next day dawned heavy and humid. The midges, those little Scottish mosquitoes, were out in force, and Patel's ran out of repellent.

Hamish returned after searching for the cat and put his gun back in the gun cabinet. Silas was sitting on the sofa with Lugs on his knee, watching television. He had a sudden feeling of malicious hatred for Silas, him with those pale-green eyes and stupid wee face and…

"What's up?" asked Silas. "You look as if you want to kill me!"

"Must be indigestion," said Hamish. "I think there's a storm coming. Thunder is in the air." But he felt as if something evil was haunting him. The cat? Rubbish. It was just a cat.

"I thought maybe you'd like a meal at the Italian's," said Silas. "My treat. Big plates o' pasta and a good night's sleep are what we need."

"Thanks," said Hamish, giving a massive shrug as if to shrug his previous awful thought away.

* * *

Silas was unused to drinking much and Hamish hardly ever got drunk, but that evening they had a bottle of wine each and ended the meal with several goblets of brandy. Silas suddenly fell asleep. Hamish thought of Maisie Walters, smug in her ministry, smug because he dare not approach her again.

He did not realise how drunk he was. He only knew the thought of Maisie getting away with murder was eating into him. Then he thought of a plan. He would smoke her out. It all seemed so logical. He called the waiter,

Willie Lamont, to bring over the wheelchair they kept in the restaurant, and together they got Silas into it. Promising to pay the bill later, Hamish wheeled Silas back to the station and dumped him on the sofa. He unlocked the gun cabinet and took out a spare untraceable phone he kept for emergencies. Just in case the call he was about to make could be traced from any of the phone towers. He got into the police Land Rover, drove to Strathbane, and parked up the road near Blair's apartment. He dialled the manse and got a sleepy and cross Maisie Walters on the phone. He switched on a machine he had once bought that disguised his voice and said, "Hamish Macbeth has just got hard evidence against you, you murdering bitch."

It was only when he rang off that he realised how very drunk he was. He drove carefully to police headquarters, parked, and fell asleep, not waking until five hours later. He drove carefully back to Lochdubh. Silas was still asleep.

Hamish groaned when he remembered that phone call. All he had done was prompt her, if she was guilty, into making sure there wasn't going to be even one little thread of evidence.

* * *

In the morning he told Silas to get ready because it was time they patrolled the villages of the west coast. All Hamish wanted to do was get clear of the station. He thought he must have run mad. Silas was looking thoroughly hung over.

As they took the coast road through Braikie, Hamish could see great heavy purple clouds massing up over the Atlantic on the west and huge glassy waves curled and smashed on the beach.

"The sea eats away more land each year," said Hamish. "The waves are getting bigger. I always feel the sea is hungry to take back the land it lost."

"Maybe if Scotland votes for independence, Sutherland might opt to join Denmark. It used to belong to the Vikings, after all."

"It's like a nightmare."

"Not as bad as that surely," said Silas. "Nice bacon."

"Not that. What I did last night."

"You mean the pair of us getting drunk?"

"Worse. I phoned up Maisie Walters and told her that Hamish Macbeth had evidence to put her in prison, something like that."

"She'll report the call and it'll be traced."

"I used a throwaway phone and phoned from Strathbane. You see, I thought that if she's innocent, she'll go straight to police headquarters and complain. If she's guilty, she might come after me. What really bothers me is that I've been building up a case against the woman when there are so many other suspects. And all built on a wee bit o' cardboard and a posh TV. You know, sometimes I'm in the same situation as one of the first coppers or detectives: only my wits to help me. They didn't even have fingerprints. I phone to ask about forensic evidence and I am told this or that person is in charge of the case and do I have their permission."

"By report, you've had one grand success rate," said Silas.

"Aye, but that was afore the cat."

"What's that got to do with it?"

"I swear that beastie scrambled my brains. I sometimes think there are things in Sutherland that are weird and don't happen anywhere else because the rock here is the oldest in the world and it is only covered with a thin layer of soil."

"You know," said Silas, "there are a lot of quite clever folk who think the earth is a living thing and is only allowing us to live on it for the moment."

Hamish laughed. "You mean I'm not the only nutcase on the planet? Let's stop at Dick's bakery and get some bacon baps for the road."

But true to form, Dick was not content until he had loaded a whole hamper into the back of the police Land Rover.

Silas had such a pleasant day that he almost regretted his decision to leave the police force until he remembered it would probably mean that dreaded transfer to Strathbane if he stayed.

CHAPTER ELEVEN

If cats looked like frogs we'd realise what nasty cruel little bastards they are.

—Terry Pratchett

A brisk breeze had made the day pleasant, but as they drove back it became close and humid. Purple clouds edged across the sky to cover the sun.

At the police station Hamish helped Silas load up the Land Rover with his personal items to take to the hotel.

"There's something bad," Silas said to him. "I didn't like to spoil the day by telling you, but I suppose I had better. Blair gave me a special phone to call him. I had it switched off but he's been trying to get me all day."

"Phone him! See if that minister's been onto Daviot."

Silas reluctantly phoned. After a few *yes, sirs* and *no, sirs*, Silas suddenly snapped, "I am leaving the force. Get yourself another patsy!" He rang off.

"Foaming at the mouth," said Silas, "but nothing about the minister."

Colonel Halburton-Smythe helped them down the stairs with Silas's belongings. He gave a little sigh as he looked around, remembering so many cosy evenings with Charlie. Silas was perhaps oversensitive for a policeman, but he recognised the loneliness mixed with diffidence in the colonel's eyes and said, "Thank you for your help. I see the place has all been cleared up. I have a bottle of wine here. Would you like a glass, sir?"

"Yes, and George is the name." With a little sigh of relief, George sank into a battered armchair.

"Hamish?" Silas held up the bottle.

"Not me. I'm off to see if I can find that cat. I'd better try to bag it and run it back to Ardnamurchan."

* * *

For some strange reason the storm did not break, although flashes of sheet lightning lit up the underside of the clouds. Hamish parked the Land Rover and then took Lugs for a walk along the waterfront. Great oily waves rolled into the loch from the Atlantic. He heard his name being called and with a feeling of gladness saw Elspeth Grant walking towards him.

"What brings you?" he cried. "What's the story?"

"I think you might be," said Elspeth. "It's weird but I am being haunted by a vision of you with your face covered in blood."

Hamish repressed a superstitious shiver. Elspeth had Gypsy blood, and some of her weird premonitions came true. "Come into the station," he said. "I was going to look for the cat but we could have a coffee first and..."

"The cat's gone!"

"Aye, and it's massacred all my poor hens."

"Okay, I'll have a coffee."

* * *

Seated in the living room, Hamish began to tell her what he had done in phoning the minster. As he discussed his reasons, he began to wonder if he had run mad.

Elspeth looked so sophisticated in designer clothes and straightened hair, it seemed to highlight the stupidity of what he had done. And yet he wished that she was the Elspeth of old with thrift shop clothes, large boots, and frizzy hair. Who wants to cuddle a fashion plate? Why did women chase after careers?

As he had stopped in mid-sentence and was staring at her blankly, Elspeth said, "What nasty thought screwed up your mind? Is it because that cat from hell is outside?"

Hamish ran out of the police station, shouting and calling. The nights were getting dark and he could not see anything at all.

He returned to join Elspeth and said crossly, "There's nothing there."

"There was," said Elspeth.

"Elspeth, it is just a cat. I know you hit the nail on the head sometimes, but it's luck, not a psychic gift. You'll be reading tarot cards next."

"Oh, go screw yourself, you pompous idiot." The last word came back to his ears from the kitchen and then was followed by the slamming of the door.

Hamish felt a wave of misery. He had fully expected to end up in bed with Elspeth as he had done sometimes before, and then all these nasty thoughts had crowded his brain.

It couldn't be anything to do with the cat. It had turned feral, yes, but it was just a cat.

The kitchen door opened just as he was making coffee, and Angela Brodie, the doctor's wife, came in.

"I was out walking," she said, "and Elspeth ran to her car as if all the hounds of hell were after her."

"Sit down. Have coffee," urged Hamish. "I felt I had done something daft to do with the murders and just as I was telling her, I got these nasty thoughts about women."

"Well, lust is a very masculine thing."

"No, sort of why don't they go back to the kitchen where they belong and have babies. That sort of mentality. Elspeth said it was the cat. I ran outside but couldn't see it. Came back in and told her she wasn't psychic and she'd be reading tarot cards next."

Angela took a mug of coffee from him and sat down at the kitchen table. "I'm not surprised she ran away. But there has always been something fey about Elspeth."

"Where's your man?"

"At a medical conference in Inverness. The writing is going badly as usual. People are always telling me that one day they will sit down and write a book as if it will all come out of a seated bum. Or they say they are going to write poetry or children's books because they want to see their printed name on the cover of something that contains as few words as possible. Have you read any of Alexander McCall Smith's books?"

"A few."

"He produces an amazing amount of books. Catherine Cookson was the same. I wish I were a compulsive writer but it all seems such an effort. Anyway, tell me what you were about to tell Elspeth."

And Hamish did, and, as he talked, he really began to get seriously worried about his mental state.

When he had finished, Angela asked, "And what had it to do with the cat?"

"She said she sensed it nearby."

"Sometimes she does come up with uncanny predictions, even when she's in Glasgow."

"I feel ashamed at having mistaken the beast for Sonsie. All I get for saving its miserable life is that it has killed all my hens."

"Could be a fox. They kill for fun."

"No, I know it's the beast. I must try to catch it and take it back to Ardnamurchan."

"Remember when I tried to keep hens and the fox kept

getting them?" said Angela. "I've still got a humane trap I got from the vet. You can borrow it if you wish."

"I'll try that," said Hamish.

* * *

He collected the trap from Angela and baited it with a piece of deer liver. He put it outside the kitchen door because he had a feeling that the animal was still roaming nearby.

He slept uneasily and then was woken at dawn by an unearthly howl. Got it, he thought, leaping out of bed.

And there was the cat in the trap, staring up at him with pure hate blazing in its yellow eyes. He suppressed a shudder and went in to change before putting the cat in the Land Rover and driving to the hotel to borrow Silas's car before heading off for Ardnamurchan. He was wearing civilian clothes, not wanting to draw too much attention to himself.

When he got there he drove to just outside the village of Kilchoan, where he knew two vets visited periodically to research. He lifted the cat in its trap down and then swore as a clawed paw lashed at his hand through the bars, drawing blood.

He fished in his pocket for a piece of paper on which he had written the Ardnamurchan number people were supposed to phone if they sighted a cat. When a man answered, Hamish said curtly, "I've left a wild cat for you just on the road outside the village." He rang off, deaf to the questions, ran for the car, and sped off. It was only when he was well clear that he realised that maybe someone could trace the owner of that trap and ask Angela so he'd better tell her to say she threw it out in the rubbish and didn't know who picked it up.

Silas came out to meet him. "I'll sleep easy knowing that cat from hell is nowhere about," he said.

"I forgot!" wailed Hamish.

"Forgot what?"

"What if that cat finds Sonsie? I should have kept my cat. I'm going back, Silas. I'll see if I can find Sonsie."

"Be careful, Hamish. There are always a lot of cameras around when they're trying to spot wildlife, and they may have your face in front of them. Leave well alone. They won't be bothered because they'll be delighted to have such a good specimen—that is, if it doesn't eat them."

"You're probably right," said Hamish sadly. "I wonder if Strathbane will replace you with anyone. The Highlands and Islands will soon be littered with my ex-coppers."

"There's a laddie joined same time as me. They call him the Fascist Pig. His real name is Johnny Southern."

"Sounds just the sort of cheil they'd inflict on me," said Hamish.

* * *

And it nearly happened. Knowing that Johnny was just the sort of policeman to make Hamish's life a misery, Blair had already put his name forward. But Johnny was a member of the Freemasons and Daviot had invited him round to his home for a glass of sherry. Johnny Southern had a square tanned handsome face and bright-blue eyes. He said wistfully that he wished to stay in Strathbane to study Superintendent Daviot's technique and learn from the master. By the end of one glass of sherry, Daviot was purring. Johnny discovered that Mrs. Daviot was almost as racist as he was himself, and when Daviot briefly left the room, he gazed into her eyes and said immigrants were a blot on the British Isles.

When Daviot came back, he asked, "If you don't go, who is there?"

"There's the Crazy Teuchter. Sorry, we all have nicknames. His real name is Freddy Ross. Real highlander," jeered Johnny Southern who came from Stirling.

"I'll have a word with him tomorrow," said Daviot.

* * *

In the following days, Hamish wished the murders were solved. He liked the police station to himself. Lugs had perked up again. The threat of that peculiar wild cat had gone. Villagers dropped in to visit once more and he realised that for quite a while they had been avoiding the station. A lot of them believed it was someone nasty who had come back as a cat.

And then Hamish had a call from Jimmy Anderson. "As Irish foreplay would say, brace yourself Bridget, your replacement for Silas should arrive today. "

"You're not allowed to make Irish jokes any more," said Hamish. "There was a lassie visiting the village and she said she was a social worker from Canada and she worked with the aborigines. I said that meant she must work in New Zealand. Not a bit of it. We were told to stop calling them Red Indians, it was now Native Americans. Well, now it is aborigines, which personally I think is a bit insulting. What's up with just calling them Americans? I don't get it. Anyway, who's this policeman they're inflicting on me?"

"New fellow called Freddy Ross. Highlander. Bit gawky but all right."

There was a knock at the kitchen door. "Bye, Jimmy, I think he's arrived."

Hamish opened the kitchen door. A tall, lanky man stood there in his uniform of regulation sweater and trousers, both looking secondhand. He had a thatch of black hair and a face like a hatchet, the sort of face you see on some puppets. He had very large hands and feet.

"Freddy Ross, reporting for duty, sir."

"Aye, bring your case in and have a seat. Coffee?"

"Yes, please, sir. I thought seeing as it's early, I got a couple of croissants from the bakery in Strathbane." He fiddled under his sweater and produced a brown paper bag.

"Thank you," said Hamish. "Now, before you settle in I would like to get one thing straight. Has Blair ordered you to spy on me?"

"I don't think anyone's told him. He wanted Johnny Southern to go and I don't think anyone has yet mentioned it's me. Why should he...? Oh, he thinks you might get a break in the murder cases and he wants to pinch anything you have. May I have some butter?"

"Certainly. Jam if you like. Where are you from originally?"

"Barra. No work there. Nothing else for me but to join the police. I am afraid, sir, that I have the grand appetite and not wanting to be a burden on your budget, I brought some things in my van. Have you a freezer?"

"Yes, out in the henhouse."

"May I suggest we put the stuff away? The sun is on my van, sir."

Hamish followed him outside. When he opened the doors of the van, Hamish said, "Have you been robbing a butcher's shop?"

There were rabbits and two hares and a whole deer carcase. "You surely haven't been poaching deer!" exclaimed Hamish.

"Roadkill," said Freddy. "Ran into me, poor beastie. Stone-dead. Glad to get a place to keep him. I'm fairly good at butchering things. If we put everything away for the moment except one rabbit, I'll make rabbit stew for our supper."

Oh, dear, thought Hamish, another foodie-copper. I wonder if he'll be any good as a policeman.

But one thing he did discover as the day drew on was that Freddy was an excellent listener. Hamish, glad to have an audience, discussed the murder cases at length as they walked around the village, and then later, as Freddy got to work in the kitchen, Hamish told him about the cat.

"People will come back, you know, sir," said Freddy. "These are the grand onions."

"Patel buys from the locals," said Hamish. "I think that cat twisted my mind because I did a daft thing."

"That being?" asked Freddy, fixing Hamish with a pair of almost hypnotic black eyes.

"It seems mad now," said Hamish, "but I was so sure that minister at Cnothan was the murderer that I disguised my voice and phoned her and said Hamish Macbeth knew she had done it and had the proof. I was hoping to draw her out but nothing happened."

"So maybe somehow she knew you weren't getting anywhere. You didn't tell anyone, did you?"

"Only Silas, the one you're replacing, and he certainly wouldn't tell anyone."

"Dinner's ready, sir."

"You may call me Hamish when we're off-duty. I've a bottle of Chablis in the fridge that I got at Patel's."

The stew was excellent. In fact, thought Hamish, if he can cook like this, it'll be another Willie, and before you know it he'll be running a restaurant.

"I noticed when we went out for a walk that you didn't lock the kitchen door," said Freddy.

"No need to."

"I was thinking. If it was me that got that phone call, I'd be terrified. I'd want to see that proof. I'd want to know what Macbeth was saying. So I wait to see him drive off. I wait until something like *Bargain Hunt* is on the telly and most folk are indoors and I nip into the station and plant a mini bug."

"I neffer thocht o' that," exclaimed Hamish, his accent becoming more sibilant in his excitement, "and it's been done before. Let's look. And if you find one, leave it where it is. Damn, if there is one she'd hear me telling Silas it was a trick. Let's try the office."

They went into the office first, running their hands along the shelves and up at the light fitting. "Nothing," said Hamish.

Freddy slouched in a corner of the office, his large hands dangling at his sides. With his beaky face, he looked so like a giant puppet that Hamish swore he could imagine strings attached.

"Everyone around told me you were a maverick," said Freddy.

"What do they mean?"

"Well, they mean you don't share your ideas with Strathbane."

"So? Strathbane wouldnae listen."

"If she heard the gossip about you, she might expect you to talk openly in the kitchen or living room. Now, me, I'd go for the kitchen."

"Let's stop talking. If we find anything, dinnae say a word," urged Hamish.

Hamish went through to the kitchen and they began to

search. But after an hour, Freddy said, "Oh, well, it was just an idea." Lugs let out a whimper.

"What's up, old boy?" asked Hamish. Lugs shuffled over and leaned against his boots. "It cannae be back," muttered Hamish.

"What can't?"

"The wild cat I took back to Ardnamurchan."

"Relax. Not a chance. Too far away."

"I'm going to nail up that flap. You look as if you've been struck by lightning. What's up?"

Freddy took out his notepad and wrote, "See that clock on the top shelf?"

"Aye, my mother gave it to me. Won it in a competition." Hamish scribbled this reply.

Freddy raised his long thin arms and lifted it down. He opened the back. He felt inside with his fingers and brought out a small, sophisticated listening device. Hamish nodded and put a finger to his lips. Freddy replaced the bug and the clock. Then they both walked outside the station.

"I was thinking that you're maybe not that bad at keeping the place clean but not perfect and what man is going to dust a clock on the top shelf—and yet the front is clean."

"You're a grand copper, Freddy," said Hamish. "Where are you from? Not Uist?"

"No, you've forgotten. Barra. Ma runs the croft with my two brothers but I wanted a change. It's lovely here. So what do we tell the bug?"

"We tell it—let me think—maybe tell it that I got the

phone out of the bog. You know, Paul's phone. I'll say I know a whiz in electronics who's just established he phoned our minister on the night of the murder. I want the glory so I'll arrest her in the morning. I'm not phoning Strathbane."

"She can't murder both of us!"

"She'll try if she's desperate. If she rigged things to make sure Mrs. Mackenzie won thon telly, it's a wonder she didn't bump her off. I mean, Mrs. Mackenzie is always yakking on about her relationship with God. You'd think her conscience would bother her. She was damn well bribed to keep her mouth shut."

"You mean, Mrs. Mackenzie knows something but so far she's not talking?"

"Exactly."

"Should we try her again?"

"No," said Hamish. "Let me think. Maybe not the phone. If she thinks there is the two of us here, she might be too frightened. I'll talk to you about coming back in the morning because you're going to Strathbane to pick up some more of your stuff this evening. I'll just say to you that I've got proof positive she's the murderer and I am going to arrest her in the morning. You ask me if I've called headquarters and I'll say that Blair would try to take the glory and I'm not having that. Can you sound natural? She'll be canny enough to know if we're faking it."

Freddy grinned. "I played Shylock in *The Merchant of Venice* at school. I was ten years old. Wanted to go on the stage."

"So why didn't you?"

"Takes money and that's what we hadn't got."

"Right," said Hamish. "Here we go. Lights, camera, action!"

They walked back into the kitchen. Hamish, sounding excited, started to talk about how he now had rock-solid proof that the minister was the murderer, and how he was going to arrest her in the morning. Freddy did his bit, ending up with saying he was off to Strathbane to pick up some stuff he had left behind but he would see Hamish at the police station in the evening.

A few hours after he had gone, Hamish said to Lugs, "Bed for us, old chap. I'll set the alarm for six in the morning. I want to catch that bitch."

CHAPTER TWELVE

Look for me by moonlight;
Watch for me by moonlight;
I'll come to thee by moonlight, though hell should bar the way!

—Alfred Noyes

Hamish would have considered himself a "new man." He was sure he regarded women as equal to men. But he did not arm himself or take any precautions as he would have done had he been waiting for a man to attack. He sat in the kitchen in the darkness. Freddy had returned and was seated beside him. Lugs lay across Hamish's boots, trembling and whimpering.

Hamish wanted to say something to comfort the dog but just in case Maisie was still at the manse, he did not want her to know he was waiting in the kitchen. He decided to lock the dog in the bedroom. Lugs would try to defend him if there was a scuffle, and he did not want him to be hurt.

Outside the kitchen window, a full moon glared down. Hamish tried hard to stay awake but his eyelids drooped and soon he was asleep. About three in the morning, he suddenly woke. The air was full of menace. He had locked the kitchen door, but he could hear scraping sounds. If she had come, she knew the key was kept up in the gutter.

The kitchen door swung open. Maisie Walters stood illuminated by a shaft of moonlight. She was holding a revolver. Hamish silently cursed his own stupidity in not having armed himself.

"Before I get rid of you," she said, flicking on the electric light and walking forward glaring at him, "tell me what you've got. Show me the proof and I'll give you a clean death. Show me nothing and it will be slow and painful."

"I haven't got a damn thing," said Hamish. "I found your listening device. I knew you'd come, you murdering bitch, if you thought I had something."

She drew out a chair on the other side of the table and sat down, but the gun in her hand never wavered.

"He deserved it," she said. "I began to wonder if it was my money he was after, because he kept saying it would be sensible if we made out our wills. I finally made out one of those do-it-yourself wills and showed it to him. In it, I'd left everything to an animal charity. He hit the roof. He said I was a sex-mad freak and he's only serviced—*serviced*—me to get some cash. I think he was mad."

"Have you a permit for that gun?" asked Hamish.

She gave a harsh cawing laugh. "If that isn't the village

bobby for you. Staring death in the face and wondering, like a petty little bureaucrat, whether I've got a permit. I neither know nor care. It belonged to my late husband. The only thing I had to comfort me were dreams of how to make him suffer. I prayed to God to smite him or to make me his instrument. Then came that phone call."

"The night you killed him?"

"Aye." Her voice rose to a mocking jeer. "'Oh darling Maisie, you've got to help me. I'm outside Mrs. Mackenzie's. I'll hide in the bushes until you come. Bring some wire clippers. That bastard copper has handcuffed me. I'm sorry I said all those nasty things.' Yakkety-yak.

"I knew about that peat bog 'cause the church has a horticultural society and we went for walks on the moors looking for lichen and mosses. Yawn. I took an old sword, a claymore, and this gun and drove down. He came out with a shit-eating grin which faded when he saw this gun. I ordered him to march and said if he yelled for help, I'd shoot his kneecaps. When we got to the bog, I told him to step in, but he started shouting that he wouldn't. I didn't want anyone hearing shots so I stabbed him in the back of the neck and he fell forward into the bog and down he went. God is good."

Mad, thought Hamish. But keep her talking.

"What about Alison? What had she done to deserve you killing her?"

"She turned up at the manse two days later saying she had heard me meeting Paul. She wanted a new car. Said she'd keep her mouth shut."

Should have noticed that new car. I'm slipping, thought Hamish bleakly. He could suddenly feel menace behind him. "Did you bring anyone with you?" he asked.

"No. I'm man enough for the both of you." Freddy was watching the gun in her hand.

"Did you rig the raffle so that Mrs. Mackenzie got the telly? Did you have to keep her quiet?"

"No, that was the kirk. They wanted a decent body for the photo. Now, you say your prayers. It's time you disappeared into the bog. March!"

This is stupid, fretted Hamish as they marched along the waterfront at gunpoint. Two policemen being taken by one woman. It's my fault. I didn't even bother to arm myself with a Taser. How did I get to be so stupid? Have I regressed? Do I think a murderess is the weaker sex? And did she try to frame Blair?

Well, I'll need to take the first bullet and save Freddy somehow.

But despite his fate, he couldn't help asking, "Why try to frame Blair? That was you, wasn't it?"

"Thought I'd give that fat pig a bad time of it."

She urged them off the road and up onto the moors. If only Freddy weren't here, thought Hamish desperately. Then I'd try to overpower her and damn the consequences. But what if she kills him? He muttered the soldier's prayer, "Oh, God, if there is a God, get me out of this."

He suddenly stopped and turned to face her. "No," he said. "You can shoot me first."

He could see Freddy getting ready to spring.

And then the air was rent by a sound that seemed to come from hell: long, wailing, primitive, and savage.

Out of the heather, on her belly, came the cat, yellow eyes blazing. The wailing stopped and was replaced by a long hissing sound. The cat sprang straight at Maisie. She let out a scream and fired and fired and fired, bullet after bullet, but the large cat sank her jaws into Maisie's neck until blood from the carotid artery poured out. Hamish wrenched the gun from her now limp hand as she fell to the ground.

* * *

Hamish sank down onto the heather. He would have liked to get the cat off Maisie's body. A murderer killed by a wild cat to save two policemen was international headlines.

"Do you want me to phone headquarters?" asked Freddy.

"No, let me think," said Hamish. "You see, I like it here. I don't want promotion. The world's press from Inverness to Hong Kong are going to be flooding into the village, and you and I will never have a quiet day again. It's a story that will never, ever go away."

Freddy sat down on the grass beside him. "When that great cat appeared, I thought I was seeing things. It looked as if it had escaped from hell."

There was a long silence. Then Hamish said cautiously, "We could tip the body and the cat's into the bog. We type up a confession, and I'll find a copy of her signature somewhere and get someone to forge it. We'll send it to Blair. I'll make sure every point is covered. Blair will be so determined to cover himself in glory that he'll go with it. When she's reported missing, headquarters won't bother much, just tell us to go and see what we can find out. That will let us into the manse to search for a signature."

"All right," said Freddy. "You're the boss. Thank goodness we're nearly at the bog. Oh, excuse me, sir." He rushed off and then Hamish could hear retching sounds.

Freddy came back. "Are you sure you are up to this, laddie?" asked Hamish.

"Aye. I'd rather it was this way than have our lives here ruined because of one horrible woman."

"Let's do it," said Hamish. First he searched her coat, and Freddy saw him slide something into his own pocket.

With the dead cat still stuck to her, they dragged Maisie's body to the peat bog and pushed it in. The sky was paling to the east. As the body sank, oily bubbles rose to the surface. Then came a sucking noise, then silence.

"I didn't think wild cats attacked humans," said Freddy.

"They don't. I don't know what that was, but you'll find out that sometimes there are more things in heaven and earth than are dreamt of outside the county of Sutherland. Now we'd better search for her car and get rid of it."

"It wasnae outside the station," said Freddy.

"I just wonder," said Hamish, "whether she might not have planned to commit suicide after she got rid of us. Let's try the cliff."

A steep cliff rose up at the sea end of the loch. What looked like Maisie's car had been driven up the path nearly to the top.

"I'll let the hand brake go and you help me push it over."

"Shouldn't we chust leave it as a sign that she meant to commit suicide?" suggested Freddy.

"Aye, maybe a good idea," said Hamish. "Leave it. I could do wi' a big ham sandwich and a cup of strong tea. I'll phone in about it while the press conference is on. But I'd better go over the kitchen wi' cleaners and scrubbers again in case the damn woman left fingerprints anywhere."

* * *

Two anxious days of waiting until at last they were ordered by headquarters to find out what had happened to Cnothan's minister. The church elder, Jake Ingles, opened the door of the manse and let them in. Hamish and Freddy snapped on latex gloves and began their search.

"Almost too easy," said Hamish, who had started searching a desk in the manse study. "There's a letter to the synod, not yet posted. I'll get a photo of the signature. Better still. She used a typewriter! You make sure no one comes in and I'll type the confession. Imagine it! In this day and age, someone using a typewriter!"

It seemed to take a long time and Freddy began to fret that they might be caught. But at last Hamish announced he was finished. "Now I need that forger."

"Sir," said Freddy cautiously, "if you use some criminal, he could blackmail you."

"Not this one. And the less you know, the better. You go back to the station and give Lugs a walk."

* * *

As he collected Lugs and walked slowly to the harbour, Freddy saw Archie Maclean talking to a beautiful blonde.

"Here's Hamish's new policeman," said Archie. "He'll tell you where he is."

She held out her hand. "I am Priscilla Halburton-Smythe. Where is Hamish?"

"Out on a missing persons case," said Freddy.

"I've been too frightened of that hell cat to go near the station. Has he got it with him?"

"No, it's gone," said Freddy. "Hamish took it to Ardnamurchan."

"Thank goodness. You are...?"

"Freddy Ross."

She smiled at him. But Freddy suddenly had a picture of all that blood and then he could almost hear the greedy sucking sounds of the bog. To Priscilla's alarm, Freddy turned white and would have fallen if she hadn't grabbed him round the waist.

"Help me get him over to the pub, Archie," said Priscilla. "A brandy's what he needs."

Archie was about to point out that hot sweet tea would

be better but then hoped that Pricilla might buy him a drink as well, so he kept quiet.

Priscilla waited until the colour had returned to his cheeks and said, "Did something frighten you?"

"Must be something I ate," said Freddy. "Hamish seems to have solved a lot of murders. Did he ever suffer from post-traumatic stress?"

"Not that I can remember," said Priscilla. "Oh, I know what it is. It's the cat, isn't it?"

"It frightened me," said Freddy, seizing on the excuse. "But it's gone now."

I wonder what Hamish really has been up to, thought Priscilla. This poor young man is a wreck.

* * *

Hamish came back in the evening. "Now we wait," he said. "Listen, Freddy, this has been a gruesome introduction to policing up here. You can get a transfer back to Strathbane if you want."

"No, there are wonderful things here," said Freddy, smiling at the memory of that golden goddess, Priscilla.

"Like what?"

But Archie had warned Freddy that although Hamish had broken off his engagement to Priscilla, he could still be made jealous, so Freddy said, "It's a grand village. Really friendly."

"I could take you to a therapist in Inverness," offered Hamish.

Freddy laughed. "I can just see it. I am upset because me

and my boss were saved from being murdered by a wild cat and we shoved the murderess and the dead cat in a peat bog. And before you know it, I'm locked up in a rubber room in some psychiatric wing."

"Oh, well, there's another kind o' therapy. We're taking a young lady out."

* * *

Freddy was disappointed to find that the young lady was a grubby schoolgirl called Fairy McSporran who seemed to have a bottomless stomach when it came to ice cream.

Anxious for another glimpse of Priscilla, Freddy suggested they call at the Tommel Castle Hotel. He said he had received relocation money and would treat Hamish to whatever he wanted. Hamish said a coffee was all he wanted, so when they arrived at the hotel, they went into the bar. Hamish stopped short and Freddy bumped into him.

Priscilla was seated at a table by the window accompanied by a tall handsome man. She waved to Hamish who went to join her. She made the introductions. Her escort was Barry fforbes. His name had two small *f*s, which he pointed out. Where on earth does she find them? marvelled Hamish.

"I see there is to be a big announcement on television," said Priscilla. "Blair is said to have found out the murderer. Press conference at six this evening."

"We'd better get back for that, Freddy," said Hamish. "Should be worth watching.

EPILOGUE

The bright face of danger
—Robert Louis Stevenson

Johnny Southern was jealous of Blair and wanted to sabotage that press conference somehow. He had heard all the stories about how Hamish Macbeth solved crimes and let someone else take the credit.

Accordingly, he plied a local newsman with drink and promises of exclusives if he would stand up at the press conference and demand to know if the rumours that Hamish Macbeth had actually solved the case were true.

Daviot, nudged by Jimmy Anderson, had suggested that they should get the signature on that confession checked in case it should prove to be a forgery. For Jimmy had an odd feeling that somehow Hamish had something to do with that confession. But Hamish was lucky in that the expert, usually highly competent, had found a letter from his wife on the dressing table, saying she was leaving him. In his subsequent distress he snapped that the letter was genuine, not even having looked at it. He spent the following days begging this wife to come home.

Blair's wife, Mary, had found him a charcoal-grey suit in an upmarket thrift shop. It fitted perfectly. He carefully put on first the white shirt with a blue stripe she had also bought him, along with a blue silk tie. As he surveyed his smart appearance in the mirror, Blair had a sudden rush of affection for his wife. "Tell you what," he said, "I'll take you to London at the end o' the month. Do some shows."

"Thanks, pet. That'll be grand," said Mary, but decided to get him to pay for everything in advance so she could take a woman friend. She was sure, after the press conference, that her husband would get roaring drunk and would have to be managed into making the bookings. When she would suggest going with a friend instead, he'd be only too glad to let her so that he could drink when and where he liked without her accusing eyes on him.

* * *

Hamish and Freddy settled in front of the television, coffee mugs in their hands and a plate of ham sandwiches on the coffee table in front of them.

Soon Blair's face seemed to fill the screen. "I have a confession here," he said portentously, "from the murderer of Paul English and Alison Ford, and the perpetrator of the murderous assault on a policeman. It comes from Mrs. Maisie Walters, minister o' the kirk." There was an unusually rewarding silence from the press as he read it out.

When he had finished, one of the reporters stood up. "Harry Girton, *Sutherland Times.* What part did Hamish Macbeth have to play in extracting this confession?"

"Who?"

"The bobby in Lochdubh."

"Nothing at all," growled Blair.

"One more question. Where did you get this confession?"

"It was sent tae me."

"So you really didn't do any detecting?" said Harry Girton. "It just landed in your lap."

Daviot stepped forward. "As Detective Chief Inspector Blair has been in charge of the case from the beginning, it is natural that the murderer, a member of the kirk, should feel he was the right man to receive her confession. That will be all."

But a reporter from the *Courier* shouted, "It could be a forgery."

"It was checked by Callum Macdonald, who is one of the foremost experts in this country, and he declares it to be genuine. That will be all."

* * *

"Well, well," said Hamish. "My wee man must be good. Callum is usually hawk-eyed. In about three-quarters of an hour's time, Jimmy Anderson will be on the doorstep. I'd better go to Patel's and buy some whisky."

"I'll go," said Freddy. "Why will he be coming?"

"Because he thinks I've got something to do with it. Don't worry. I've bunged another forged note off to Blair. I let myself into the manse last night and typed one out and got the signature forged."

"And what does it say?"

"I have sinned in the eyes of the Lord. I send my body to the depths of the ocean from the top of the cliff at Lochdubh and may God have mercy on my soul."

"Don't you feel a bit blasphemous, Hamish?"

"Not a bit of it."

* * *

Freddy strolled into Patel's grocery-*cum*-post-office shop. The sun was shining outside on the loch, and a brisk breeze was blowing from the Atlantic. He suddenly realised why it was that Hamish Macbeth would do everything in his power to make sure he was kept on in Lochdubh. Various villagers greeted him and welcomed him to the village. The Currie sisters had seen him approaching the shop and had rushed home to return and give him a plate of their famous scones. Archie Maclean gave him a couple of mackerel and asked him if he would tell Hamish that a man over at Bonar Bridge had hens for sale. Freddy paid for the whisky and as he left the shop, he saw Priscilla hurrying along the waterfront. As she came closer, he saw she had been crying.

"Oh, hullo," she said and then she began to weep.

"Oh, dear," said Freddy. "Come to the station."

"No, I don't want to see Hamish!"

"Well, now. We'll chust get into ma old banger of a car and take off. There's a wee tea shoppie on the Lairg road. Nothin' like strong tea and cream cakes to settle a body."

Unresisting, Priscilla allowed herself to be helped into Freddy's old car. Freddy drove off feeling like a knight of old who had just rescued the princess.

* * *

Hamish looked at the clock. What was keeping Freddy? He was about to go and search for him when Jimmy arrived.

"Where's the hooch?" he cried, slumping down at a chair at the kitchen table.

"Freddy went to Patel's to buy some and he hasnae come back. Oh, I've remembered. I've got a bottle of brandy in the back of the bedroom cupboard along wi' the medical supplies."

"Then wheel it out!"

"Okay. I'll phone Patel's first to see if anyone's seen Freddy."

After five minutes Hamish came back with the brandy. "You took your time," grumbled Jimmy as Hamish poured him a measure.

"Checking up on Freddy. He took off with Priscilla. Why?"

"Phone him. He's got a mobile, hasn't he?"

"It's his day off and he's a grown man. None of my business."

"I'll tell you what's my business," said Jimmy. "Why do I have this feeling that it's all too simple? And I get to thinking. Up in Lochdubh, there's a clever copper who doesn't want promotion and so he gets a confession and bungs it off to Blair."

"It is the grand imagination you have there, Jimmy."

"Now, here's an odd thing. I go to see that elder o' the kirk, Jake Ingles, and he tells me that Maisie got a call from someone saying Hamish Macbeth knew she was the murderer and had the proof. So I get to thinking that Macbeth is playing the sacrificial goat and trying to lure her into the open. So maybe he does. And maybe kills her. But why hush it up? And where's that cat from hell that was terrifying the village? And that expert on forgery? His wife's left him and now he's drunk the whole time. He wouldn't know a forgery from his arsehole at the moment. What I'm saying is this. Before I get that so-called confession down to Glasgow to another expert, what do you have to say, and pour another shot for me while you speak."

"Leave it, Jimmy, the murder is solved," said Hamish.

"No, laddie. If you've solved the case and given the credit to Blair, at least you might ha' given it to me."

"And you'd have seized it with both hands and not asked

questions? You're too good a detective. So what are you going to do? Find that other expert? Blow the case wide open? Daviot will hate you, Blair will hate you. Our forgery expert might just stick to his guns, not wanting to ruin his reputation."

"Is she dead?"

"Yes."

"You killed her?"

"No, I... Who the hell is that?"

The kitchen door opened and Jake Ingles burst in. "I never would have believed her so evil," he cried, waving a black leather-bound notebook.

"Come in and sit down. Now what is this?" asked Hamish, while all the time he was praying that Jimmy would not betray him.

"The new minister didnae like that desk o' Maisie's so I said I'd chop it up for firewood because no one would buy an old shabby thing like that. When I took the axe to it, a wee secret drawer pops out and I read all this filth she had written."

"Pour him a brandy, Jimmy," said Hamish, "while I hae a look."

"Pour it yourself," snapped Jimmy. "I'll look at it."

He read carefully, muttering, "Mad. Quite mad. Thinks God was telling her to do the murders. Says she'll commit one more and then go to join Paul in the bog. Mr. Ingles, I'll give you a receipt for this. In the name o' the wee man. I'll call my own press conference and get the digger up to the bog." Then he muttered, "This is all mine, Hamish."

* * *

When Freddy came back, he found Hamish on his own in the kitchen. Priscilla had urged Freddy not to tell Hamish what had upset her, although Freddy was still puzzled as to why this goddess had been so upset when a man she had invited up to Scotland had only tried to kiss her. Rape he could have understood. But Hamish blurted out all about the notebook and the real confession.

Freddy looked relieved. "We're covered then," he said.

"No. In her confession, she says she's going to throw herself in the bog. Jimmy is getting it excavated. Peat protects bodies. She'll be brought up with that cat at her neck and every sign that the cat killed her. The world's press will descend on us."

They had not noticed how dark it had been getting outside, and both jumped nervously when a great crash of thunder shook the station. Then came the relentless drumming of rain on the roof. Freddy put the bottle of whisky on the table. He looked enquiringly at Hamish, who shook his head and put the kettle on for coffee. Outside the terrifying winds of Sutherland rose high and higher, crashing and booming. "Let's see if Jimmy's got his press conference," said Hamish going into the living room, only to find there was a power cut.

"What can we do?" shouted Freddy above the noise of the storm. Hamish shook his head. The kettle he had put on top of the wood-burning stove began to whistle.

He retreated to the kitchen, made two cups of coffee, and opened a tin of shortbread which had a picture on the lid of a blonde and blue-eyed Bonnie Prince Charlie waving a sword.

The thunder rolled away but still the wind howled and the old police station seemed to shake to its very foundations. Then as if Thor and his hordes had at last ridden away, the roar of the storm slowly subsided, and bit by bit the rain stopped.

Hamish's hazel eyes began to gleam. "Thon peat bog'll be filled to overflowing with the rain. I'm going up there to see if she floats to the top. All I want to do is get the cat off her. You can stay here, Freddy."

"No, I'll come with you. It's time I hardened up."

They walked quickly on foot up onto the moors. Grateful for the springy heather underfoot which stopped them from sinking into the mud, they made their way to the peat bog. Water was overflowing around it, but no signs of anything coming to the top. Freddy had brought along a long shepherd's crook. He fished in the bog with the crook end. "Got something," he whispered, his face turning greenish white in the pale evening sunlight which had followed the storm.

"Give me the crook," said Hamish, "and go and sit on that rock over there."

Freddy nodded dumbly and did as he was told.

Hamish gave a massive tug and then, with a gurgling plop, something came free and sailed over his head. He turned and looked behind him. It was the wet muddy corpse of the cat.

He fished in the bag he had brought with him, took out a sack, and put the cat into it. He could not believe this horrible creature was actually dead.

"Come on, Freddy. It is as dead as a doornail and there will be no great story. I've something else. She had a knife in her pocket, and before we chucked her in the bog I wiped her blood on it. There'll be her blood in the cracks round the handle and with any luck they might think she cut her own throat." He threw the knife into the bog and, followed by Freddy, made his way back to the police station.

"Where will you bury the beast?" asked Freddy.

"I'll chuck it in the loch. Look, Freddy, make yourself some strong tea. I'll do this."

Hamish went down to the harbour and unhitched one of the rowing boats that Archie hired out to the tourists. In the middle of the loch, he took out the body of the cat. He began to pile some rocks he had picked up into the bag, and then, grabbing the cat by the scruff of the neck, he began to stuff it in. That was when one eye appeared to open and glare at him with a yellow light. He screamed with fright and then realised it was the late sun shining on one of the dead cat's eyes.

He let out a slow sigh of relief as he hurled the bag over the side and watched it sink.

* * *

Hamish and Freddy both woke late the next morning, roused by someone banging on the kitchen door. Hamish wrapped himself in his old tatty tartan dressing gown and went to answer it. Jimmy Anderson stood there, grinning from ear to ear.

"Man, I am the hero o' the hour. Got her body. Don't know why the silly moo thought she was joining Paul English when she must ha' known we got him up and out the bog ages ago. She'd cut her own throat and made a right mess o' it. Anyway, plaudits for me. Blair in a flaming temper. Big yins from Glasgow murmured congratulations and took the next plane south. Hey, I thought thon cat had gone."

"It has," said Hamish, feeling his stomach lurch. "Why?"

"Dunno. Feel it around. Where's the celebration drink?"

"Isn't it too early?"

"While you've been lying in the arms o' Murphy, the clock's been whizzing around. It's eleven in the morning and the sun is over the yardarm, not to mention pooping on the poop deck, so let's have it."

Freddy had joined them to hear the last sentence. "I put the whisky from yesterday in the cupboard over the stove."

"Bring it out, lad. Are you sure that damn cat isn't somewhere around? The whole place smells o' wet cat. Hey! Look out!"

Hamish caught Freddy as he collapsed in a dead faint. "I think he's been overdoing it," he said, easing the policeman's limp body onto a kitchen chair and slapping his cheeks.

Hamish found a little brandy left from before and got Freddy to drink some. "Go and lie down," urged Hamish. "I'll take you to the doctor later." He helped Freddy to bed and came back to find Jimmy cradling a large glass of whisky in his hands.

"Well, here's tae me," said Jimmy, taking a gulp. "Your lad there was romancing Miss Priscilla over the teacups all afternoon while we were waiting for the whisky."

"I know about that," said Hamish, somehow anxious not to betray that it was the first he'd heard of this tea party. "Priscilla's aye been kind to newcomers. But I don't think Freddy's up to policing."

"You don't want him, we'll take him back."

"No, he'd hate that. I'll think of something." Hamish felt a surge of dislike for Freddy. If he went on fainting all over the place, then one day he was going to open his mouth and tell someone everything. And what the hell had he been doing with Priscilla?

* * *

Blair was consumed with fear and hatred. He was sure it was Hamish who was behind the finding of that first confession. All his old hatred for Hamish came back and he began to plot and plan ways to get rid of him. Also, with all his old detective intuition which was always there, despite being blurred a bit by booze, he had *smelled* that there was something wrong with that first confession.

The weak link between falsehood and truth might lie with Freddy. But he would have to get Freddy alone. He phoned the station, and it was Jimmy who answered. He told Blair that Hamish had said he was going to spend the day on his extensive beat; Freddy was to stay behind and answer the phone. Blair thanked him and then set out for Lochdubh.

Crouched over the wheel of his car, he muttered, "I'll beat the shit out of that copper until I get the truth."

* * *

But while he was on the road to Lochdubh, Priscilla called at the station to thank Freddy for his listening ear and warm sympathy. She was used to men fancying her as some sort of arm candy and none of them had ever wanted to comfort her or listen to her, although a treacherous voice was whispering that Hamish had done his best while they were engaged. The fact was, she had something more to trouble her: Clarry, the cook, had fallen ill with gallstones and was in Braikie hospital, leaving the hotel with the incipient visit of twelve members of the famous Gourmet Club. The head of the club was a waspish man who would give the restaurant a bad report out of spite because the actual planned gourmet lunch had been cancelled.

Freddy listened carefully and then said, "I think I could do that. I'm a good cook, though I say it myself. Let's go to the hotel kitchen. I'll do my best."

While Priscilla drove him to the hotel, Freddy took out

his iPad and Googled the name of the head of the Gourmet Club, Peregrine Wimple. He decided that the presentation of the food must be pretentious in the extreme.

* * *

Blair's wife, Mary, had followed him in her car. She reflected bitterly that a lot of her life was taken up these days with keeping her husband out of the asylum. She had heard him talking in his sleep and knew he was out for revenge. She kept well back on the road, not wanting her husband to see her.

They were about to pass the entrance to the Tommel Castle Hotel when Blair slammed on the brakes. The car park was visible from the road, and he had spotted Freddy's old car.

Worse and worse, thought Mary as she eventually cruised along to the hotel entrance and saw her husband's car. What was he after? Hamish's police Land Rover wasn't there. Blair had been grinding his teeth in his sleep and muttering, "I'll beat it out o' him." Mary didn't think he'd take on Hamish in a fight. But what about Hamish's new policeman, Freddy something-or-other?

* * *

Priscilla was in the kitchen, gazing in wonder at the trays of starters being conjured up under Freddy's clever fingers. There were radishes like rosebuds, decorating small side bowls of salad; vols-au-vent filled with prawns Marie Rose; Orkney scallops on beds of samphire; and wild smoked salmon rolled up with a small bowl of real mayonnaise on each plate.

She was just beginning to say, "You're a genius..." when the kitchen door was hurled open and Blair, his face purple with rage and the desire for revenge, stood on the threshold.

"You! Oot," he snarled at Freddy.

"Leave him alone!" shouted Priscilla, stepping in front of Freddy.

Blair made the awful mistake of thinking he was just tugging Priscilla aside but he jerked at her arm so hard that she went flying and crashed into the cooker.

Freddy saw his golden goddess assaulted and was consumed with such rage that he threw a massive punch that sent Blair flying off back through the kitchen door to drop unconscious at the feet of his horrified wife.

The ambulance was called but Blair had recovered consciousness to find himself in deep trouble. Daviot had been sent for and arrived by helicopter. Priscilla explained that Freddy had been helping out as part of a police initiative to provide help in the community. Silas stayed hidden in his basement apartment. The last thing he wanted was to bring himself to the attention of police headquarters even though he had left. He thought he would never forget his awful experiences while policing for Hamish.

Nobody could raise Hamish. He was not answering his mobile or the police radio.

Daviot was wondering what on earth to do about Blair. He feared that the detective still had incriminating photos of his wife. A few years ago she had been drugged and photographed in compromising positions. Hamish had told him he had recovered them all, but Blair claimed otherwise. At last Daviot had an idea. "It is either a transfer to Glasgow," he said, "or the sack."

"I'll take the transfer," mumbled Blair. Mary brightened. Glasgow! Shops! Theatres! Now if her husband would just go back to being a nasty drunk. That, she could handle.

* * *

Peregrine Wimple was impressed but determined not to show it. He liked to keep a faint sneer on his face to frighten restaurateurs waiting for his lordly verdict. It takes a snob to know one. So George Halburton-Smythe, coached by his daughter, leaned over Peregrine and said confidentially, "I can see you appreciate good food. You can always tell one of those lower-class pseuds. Always poking at stuff on their plate and sneering."

He then moved out of the dining room and said to his daughter, "I hope I memorised all you told me to say."

"He's actually smiling, the little ponce. What are we to do about Freddy? He hates the police."

"Can't afford two chefs."

"Hamish will think of something. He always does," said Priscilla. "Oh, where *is* Hamish?"

* * *

Hamish had spent the day just outside the reserve at Ardnamurchan. He had cooked venison sausages, Sonsie's favourite. It was only a faint hope, he thought with a sigh, as he packed up the sausages for Lugs. He had left the dog at the station.

He decided to call at Braikie hospital before going home to see how Clarry was getting on. The ex-policeman looked wanly at Hamish. "I've never been so sick of water in ma life," he said. "Fine goings-on at the hotel."

"What's going on?" asked Hamish and then listened in amazement to the tale of Blair's attack.

When Clarry had finished, Hamish said, "Well, you've still got your job. I thought for a moment I was going to lose another copper to food."

"I've a wee bittie o' a problem," said Clarry, fishing a letter out from under his pillow. "This is from Acme Television. One o' the producers spotted me when he was on holiday. They want me to be a TV chef. The pay's great. I've got the wife and kids to think of. They think the highland accent'll go down well."

"I'll talk to Freddy," said Hamish. "He doesnae like policing any more."

* * *

Hamish drove slowly home. A happy Freddy would not talk. But if he continued to be a policeman and there was another gruesome case, then he might snap.

All I need, thought Hamish, is a wee bit o' luck.

He parked the Land Rover at the side of the police station. Lugs came hurtling through the flap, barking excitedly and jumping up and down.

"I'd like to think the welcome was for me," said Hamish, "but you smell the sausages."

He opened the back of the Land Rover and a wild cat leapt to the ground and then up into Hamish's arms. He stared at the creature in wonder. "Sonsie!" he said.

He carried the large cat indoors, marvelling that he could ever have mistaken that creature from hell as Sonsie.

* * *

To her irritation, Priscilla, about to call on Hamish later that evening, found she was joined by Elspeth Grant. The rumour in the village was that Hamish had proposed marriage to Elspeth but that Elspeth refused to leave Glasgow. Freddy was cleaning up at the hotel and Priscilla wanted to talk over his problem with Hamish, because Freddy had said he would rather work at the hotel than be a policeman. Priscilla found herself wishing that Elspeth would go away.

The kitchen door was open. The sound of the television came from the living room.

Together they looked into the room.

Hamish Macbeth lay stretched out on the sofa, Sonsie draped over his chest and Lugs at his feet. He had a half smile on his face.

Both women turned and walked silently outside, over to the waterfront, and leaned on the wall.

"That's that, then," said Elspeth. "No woman alive is ever going to compete with that cat!"

* * *

One last fine day before the very end of summer and Archie Maclean was dreading his latest passengers. He had been contracted to take a party of primary school children on a trip round the loch, children from the tower blocks of Strathbane, children with feral faces, old before their time. Evil, that's what they are, thought Archie, just like that damn cat. Then he had an idea. He cut the engine, remembering the boat was now right over where Hamish had told him he had got rid of the cat.

He fished up an old loud-hailer and yelled into it. "If yis'll gaither round, I'll tell you about the Mooley Cat what came from hell and is right under us the noo. Ice cream for the ones that stay quiet. None for the ones who cannae listen."

They all fell quiet, to his amazement. And so Archie began, "Once upon a time…" He had the true highlander's gift of the gab. Why he'd decided to call it the Mooley Cat, he never knew. He had just got to the bit where that brave policeman, Hamish Macbeth, had shot the beast from hell with a silver bullet when, from the suddenly dark sky above, lightning stabbed down into the loch and the children clutched each other and screamed.

Word spread far and wide and Archie found he had to extend his season as people clambered aboard, searching for places and waiting to hear the story.

To the villagers, the cat began to seem like a bad dream, something thought up by Archie. And with his new wealth, no more was Mrs. Archie allowed to boil his clothes in the copper. He bought her the latest in washing machines and himself a new skipper's cap and a denim jacket and jeans.

Only Freddy sometimes thought he heard a cat howl at night and put the pillows over his head and lay there shaking.

* * *

Hamish Macbeth made a trip to Glasgow and proposed marriage to Elspeth Grant. But she looked at him sadly and said he had a wife already called Sonsie.

Returning to his station and feeling low, Hamish suddenly saw a policewoman standing outside. Her figure in her smart uniform was perfect. The glossy waves of her black hair showed under her cap. Her eyes were large and blue in a perfect oval of a face.

"Constable Dorothy McIver reporting for duty," she said.

Hamish grinned. He had a feeling that something good had come his way at last.

About the Author

M. C. Beaton has won international acclaim for her *New York Times* bestselling Hamish Macbeth mysteries, and the BBC has aired twenty-four episodes based on the series. Beaton is also the author of the bestselling Agatha Raisin novels, which aired as an eight-episode dramatic series on PBS, starring Ashley Jensen. M. C. Beaton's books have been translated into seventeen languages. She lives in the Cotswolds. For more information, you can visit MCBeaton.com.